We'll to the Woods
No More

Nous n'irons plus au bois
Les lauriers sont coupés . . . .

WE'LL TO THE WOODS NO MORE

EDOUARD DUJARDIN

An introduction by Leon Edel
A translation by Stuart Gilbert
Illustrations by Alice Laughlin

NEW DIRECTIONS

Manufactured in the United States of America. New Directions books are
printed on acid-free paper. First published clothbound by New Directions in
1938; reissued clothbound with introduction by Leon Edel in 1957; reissued
as New Directions Paperbook 682 in 1990. Published simultaneously in
Canada by Penguin Books Canada Limited.

Library of Congress Cataloging-in-Publication Data

Dujardin, Edouard, 1861–1949. [Lauriers sont coupés. English]
We'll to the woods no more / Edouard Dujardin ; an introduction by Leon
Edel ; a translation by Stuart Gilbert ; illustrations by Alice Laughlin.
        p.   cm.   Translation of: Les lauriers sont coupés.
                ISBN 0-8112-1113-4 (pbk. : alk. paper)
                        I. Title.
PQ2220.D8L313   1990   89-13019
843'.6—dc20   CIP

New Directions Books are published for James Laughlin
by New Directions Publishing Corporation,
80 Eighth Avenue, New York 10011

DÉDICACE

Ma jeunesse qui cherchait un signe dans le passé
a dédié son espérance à Racine
un grand nombre d'années ont traversé l'horizon
et j'ai vu le signe apparaître aux portes de l'avenir
mon espérance je la dédie aujourd'hui
à JAMES JOYCE
au glorieux nouveau-venu
au suprême romancier d'âmes

E. D.

1930

Introduction

We'll to the Woods No More is a slender novel—
its French title is *Les lauriers sont coupés*—
written in the Paris of the 1880's and promptly
forgotten, as so many books are, only to be
revived in our century under strange and rather
charming circumstances—and for good reason.
Taken by itself, it is a minor piece of fiction;
not a few readers, casting a cursory glance at
it, would call it "trivial." And trivial it doubt-
less is, if we insist on reading only "great
books"—if we think we must sojourn per-
petually among the mountain-tops of literature.

Let us begin, then, by saying that *We'll to
the Woods No More* is neither a "great book,"
nor a "best book," nor even a misunderstood
book. It was for a long time simply a neglected
book. It came into being in a Paris much pre-

occupied with *naturalisme*. Zola was the major figure. The deterministic novel he fathered, with its emphasis on document, on popularized Darwin, on journalism, held sway. Or, Frenchmen were reading the since out-dated and airless novels of Paul Bourget, or enjoying Maupassant's admirably-realized "slices of life." A slender novel which was neither a document nor a slice of life, which belonged to the Symbolist revolt against naturalism, could hardly expect to make an impression among more strident voices. The Symbolists and the Impressionists were of the avant-garde. Flaubert was but seven years dead and Wagner was the rage of the French salons. At least a quarter of a century was to elapse before these new movements would be fully understood and appreciated; it usually takes that much time for the avant-garde to become the rear-guard.

But Symbolism was more than avant-garde. It was the dawn of twentieth century literature. One of the minor Symbolists was Édouard Dujardin, a young music critic, an impassioned Wagnerian. In 1887 he started serializing *Les lauriers sont coupés* in *La Revue Indépendante*, and it was read with interest by his fellow-Symbolists and his friend George Moore, then in his naturalist phase. If one reads it today for "story" it proves to be an agreeable little diversion—perhaps because of the honesty with which the situation is told: a young-man-about-town wants to sleep with a Parisian actress; she puts him off, but does not hesitate to take money from him. Presently he is paying her bills. And on the one evening of the novel he thinks that perhaps, finally, she will be his. Related in this way nothing could be more banal. Yet the dew of early morning has been sprinkled over the banalities. The writing is fresh and imaginative. The book possesses, above all, a focused vividness which its early readers recognized. When we ask ourselves how a tale so hackneyed can be so vivid, we discover that our interest is held by the way in which the story is told. This is what James Joyce recognized; years later he praised the book because the reader is "from the very first line posted within the mind of the protagonist." We might add that he remains posted there to the very last line.

We'll to the Woods No More represents, thus, in its way, a small triumph of method over matter: it might be argued that the triumph is one of poetry over prose. However that may be, it is the rare and beautiful case of a minor work which launched a major movement.

For Édouard Dujardin's novel inaugurated nothing less than the era of the *monologue intérieur*, thereby altering the temporal and spatial form of the modern novel. I recognize that these are empyreal words, atmospheric and Einsteinian, and that they figure strangely in discussion of a work bounded by the boulevards and placed in the consciousness of a self-obsessed Parisian dandy. What, the reader may ask, has the chase after an actress to do with matters dimensional and horological? Certainly, Édouard Dujardin, scribbling his novel in 1887 (one imagines his pointed beard held high in the air, a flower in his buttonhole, a long-stemmed cigarette holder in his mouth), was conscious of little but the difficulties of the literary "stunt" he had set himself. He would write a novel wholly subjective. He would

never go "outside" his character's mind. It
would all take place in a single evening, a
matter of hours—all thought and no action.
The novel ran its course in the magazine,
appeared as a volume, attracted little notice,
and then faded away. A decade later Dujardin
reprinted it as the title story in a collection
of his prose and verse, and it was this edition,
apparently, which James Joyce came upon, after
the century's turn, and read during his trip
from Paris to Dublin in 1902—the troubled
journey commemorated in the opening pages of
Ulysses. Twenty years later the Irish novelist
still remembered the book and could pay trib-
ute to it as the principal source for is stream-
of-consciousness techniques in his Dublin Odys-
sey.

Édouard Dujardin was still alive when Joyce
invoked his name. In literary obscurity, he was
writing books on religion and on music. He
responded with almost pathetic gratitude to
the greatness which the author of *Ulysses* thrust
upon him. This was indeed a case of *Lazar veni
foras;* and if Dujardin evoked the image of himself as one raised from the dead, in a flattering

re-dedication of a new edition of his book (it was of 1924), he was well aware that by implication he was calling Joyce the Christ who had performed the miracle. The allusion was hardly lost upon the fabulous artificer. With that ironic modesty which was the mask of his self-assertion, he responded by inscribing a copy of *Ulysses* to the "preacher of the inner word" from the "impenitent thief." The gallantries of the occasion were properly observed.

Around these, however, a serious debate had developed. What was the *monologue intérieur?* How "new" was it? How was it to be defined? In due course Dujardin was invited to Germany to lecture on his "discovery." At Berlin, Marburg, Leipzig, during the dying days of the Weimar Republic, he delivered a rambling discourse, later printed, which bore the portentous title *Le monologue intérieur, son apparition, ses origines, sa place dans l'oeuvre de James Joyce et dans le roman contemporain.* This sounds like a formidable treatise. The title of the lecture no doubt had appeal in a country where the higher scholarship has always cultivated the higher pedantry. Dujardin, moreover, knew his Germany and may have assumed a certain Teutonic tone in his old age which his younger self would have repudiated, although he had been a "Perfect Wagnerite," in the early days of Bayreuth. It was indeed Wagner's music, so much in vogue among the Parisian Symbolists, which had suggested to him the idea for his work. In tracing his inner monologue of the Parisian dandy, Dujardin sought to capture the *leit-motifs* of consciousness, the orchestra of the inner man. The Dujardin discourse makes strange reading today. It is a farrago of self-laudation, a *potpourri* of quotations from reviewers, reminiscences, literary history, and now and again a kind of blinking search to define, in the bright light of 1930, the old candle-light intuition of 1887. The lecture reads as if Dujardin arrived at his theories from his perusal of *Ulysses*, rather than from a rereading of *Les lauriers sont coupés*.

The most valuable part of the Dujardin lecture is his attempt to define inner monologue. The *monologue intérieur*, he says, is "in its nature on the order of poetry," by which he means that it describes reflection, abstraction, momentary impression, mood, tone, rather than narrates action; it is that "unheard and unspoken speech by which a character expresses his inmost thoughts." In this he seemed to be characterizing little more than Hamlet's soliloquies, or those passages of subjective reflection which Tolstoy brilliantly introduced in *War and Peace*, or the ruminations of Dostoevsky's driven personages. Dujardin went on to say, however, that the "inmost thoughts" have to be those "lying nearest the unconscious," and they must be recorded "without regard to logical organization." In the Dujardin theory, this can be accomplished only "by means of direct sentences reduced to syntactic minimum," set down "in such a way as to give the impression of reproducing the thoughts just as they come into the mind." Dujardin was describing what he had tried to do, what Joyce had accomplished.

Dujardin's claims failed to impress many critics. They could see no distinction between inner monologue, as he described it, and the time-tested soliloquies of the stage. Dujardin himself does not seem to have understood—as Joyce did—the new dimensions involved in his experiment. It was not only that the story was being told from the "inside out," but that from the moment this was done a significant change took place in the relationship between author and reader. For one thing, both were committed to the single "point of view" after the manner of Browning's dramatic poems or the experiments Henry James had begun to carry out in his fiction. The mind or consciousness of the protagonist was made to narrate itself, as a play does on the stage. The reader was no longer being given an organized, explained story, but by being posted in the character's mind could see, think, know only as much as was in the character's consciousness, received the sensory stimuli of that personage and was assimilated into the fictional mind, its scrambled past and present, its dislocations of time and space. The story was no longer saying "Once upon a time . . ."—it was saying "I remember the time when . . ." And the reader was present at the instant of memory.

In addition to committing the reader to a

specific angle of vision and the thoughts "just as they come into the mind," this type of fiction made him aware of experience as simultaneous rather than consecutive. Flaubert, earlier in the century, had shown in a single memorable scene how this could be done by a writer even though in the literary art one must use words consecutively and cannot blend them into simultaneity as the composer does his instruments in the orchestra. The scene was that of the village fair in *Madame Bovary*. There was a distinct foreshadowing of cinema in the way Flaubert made the reader's eyes travel over street and square, return to the window overlooking the scene, come back to the platform, and listen *at the same time* both to the oratory of the fair filled with political clichés, and the romantic clichés being exchanged by Emma and Rodolphe. This was a striking instance of literary *montage* long before it had been thought of as possible on the screen. The reader is asked, as Joseph Frank has suggested, to move his head from side to side, as at a tennis match, if he is to take in the entire scene. This is being done constantly for the spectator at a movie. Cinema consists, after all, of bits and pieces of reality, strung together to give an illusion of continuity, "stills" flashed before us at such a speed that we have a sense of motion and wholeness—a horse galloping, a close-up of the horse's hoofs, a close-up of the rider in the saddle, a shot of the horse within the landscape. Flashed before us in that order the separate pictures become one picture in the spectator's mind, the disparate moments merge into a continuum. "The imitation of life through the medium of language has never been undertaken more literally," Harry Levin wrote discussing *montage* as Joyce used it. "*Ulysses* ignores the customary formalities of narration and invites us to share a flux of undifferentiated experience. We are not told how the characters behave; we are confronted with the *stimuli* that affect their behavior, and expected to respond sympathetically. The act of communication, the bond of sympathy which identifies the reader with the book, comes almost too close for comfort."

Mallarmé had, before Joyce, grasped the essence of Dujardin's experiment. The phrase he pronounced after reading *Les lauriers sont coupés* is unforgettable: *l'instant pris à la gorge.*

The moment seized by the throat! The image
is as striking as it is violent. Mallarmé visioned
the capture of time as a process of placing vigor-
ous poetic hands upon the moment, if he could
but get them around its elusive velvety throat.
The violence of the image suggests his frustra-
tion. William James, who coined the meta-
phor *stream-of-consciousness*, found equally poetic
ways of describing evanescence: trying to
capture a thought as it occurs, he wrote, was
like turning on the light to look at the darkness,
or enclosing a snowflake in the palm of one's
hand. Proust sought to seize the moment by
other means: he caressed and cherished it,
experienced it to the full and then recaptured,
in memory, the color and perfume with which
it was charged. Virginia Woolf reached out for
it with a kind of anguish of intensity, seeing it
as the flare and flicker of a match which the
darkness must extinguish and which must be
replaced by another flicking and flaring match,
so that life becomes a continuity of extinctions.
Dujardin, proceeding by intuition, does not

seem to have pondered the matter. He simply attacked his problem with the optimism of his youth, and the sense of an indoctrinate Symbolist convinced that words can be made to do anything:

. . . time and place come to a point; it is the Now and Here, this hour that is striking all around me life . . .

So day-dreams Daniel Prince in the novel's opening lines and very promptly we have been placed in his world. The reader ceases to be himself. He takes over the character's thoughts; he does not receive them at second hand from the novelist. Time is present and vertical, not historical and horizontal. The intensities of feeling are no longer conveyed as of the past: *they are being experienced as they occur.* It is "the Now and Here." The sense of distance, which exists in James, which Conrad cultivated, has been completely removed.

To read Dujardin today out of his chronological place in literary history can still be an engrossing process even though we have read the works of those who learned from him.

For we watch Dujardin at grips with his self-created dilemma, persisting with the determination of a pioneer. Suddenly he is floundering. He doesn't know how to graft memories of the past into the consciousness of the moment. Unable to melt his data into the inner monologue of Daniel Prince, he falls back on tried letter-diary devices and we are back in the days of Choderlos de Laclos or Samuel Richardson. Daniel Prince rereads old letters; he reads journals; the flow of the monologue is arrested for many pages while the past is reread. Yet if there has been regression, it has occurred in the interest of not betraying the experiment. We learn what has gone before. This done, we move forward again in Daniel Prince's consciousness and into the evening's denouement. Throughout the novel, however, Dujardin is struggling with still another problem. What is he to do with descriptive detail, that sense of immediate material things of which Balzac made fiction singularly aware? How describe the room, the street, the house and still remain "inside" Daniel Prince? Later writers solved this problem in many ways, but in 1887 Dujardin breathlessly moves an excessive quantity of furniture into the consciousness of his personage. The effect is often curious:

The hour is striking six, the hour I waited for. Here is the house I have to enter, where I shall meet someone; the house, the hall; let's go in.

Four decades later he might have allowed a bell to strike the hour for him, or revealed it through the glimpse of a clock-face. He would have understood that we enter houses and halls without semaphoring these to ourselves, that we do not mystify ourselves by saying, "I shall meet someone," but know, when we have an appointment, that the "someone" has a face, a name, characteristics by which he is fixed in our mind.

It is easy, however, to criticize Dujardin from our Joycean hindsight. What we must remember is the staunch, pioneer strength of *We'll to the Woods No More* and we must recognize as well, the beauty of certain of the writer's evocations. The reader who estab-lishes rapport with Daniel Prince is in Paris in 1887. Suddenly he is aware of the soft evening, not because Dujardin has described it, but because he feels the air on his face; he is sauntering along the boulevards with top hat and gloves, or is in the carriage with Leah, or gaping at the well-dressed women, lighting a candle in his dressing room, splashing water on his face, standing on the balcony picking out the pictures of the night: the grey-black sky, the blue tiny stars "like tremulous drops of water," while all around there is the misty impressionist paleness of open sky, lighted windows, the "solid gloom of trees." Poetic fancy comes to the aid of Dujardin and he is the confirmed Symbolist: language evokes his atmosphere and it is essentially the atmosphere of the mind.

Once Dujardin had shown the way, this atmosphere was to be evoked in fiction by many writers. Sometimes, as in the streams-of-consciousness of *Ulysses*, it is to give the effect of an inner life of flotsam and jetsam: the data of experience jumbled for the reader as any moment of our day can be a jumble. Sometimes, as in Molly Bloom's soliloquy, it is stream-of-consciousness from which external stimuli have been largely filtered out, so that we have an inner monologue constructed of verbal associations. Sometimes, as in Virginia Woolf, the writer chooses a personal unvarying poetic medium, and weaves an inner monologue out of moments of perception, glimpsed experiences by which we are made to feel subjective life without the Joycean weight of detail. And sometimes it becomes the bold experimentation of Faulkner, who undertakes to convey the subterranean life of persons lacking words to express feeling, someone as inarticulate as Benjy Compson, the idiot, whose consciousness is beyond record, for he can neither think nor communicate: he can only feel—and bellow. In his case Faulkner performs one of the most humane and beautiful functions of the poet: he provides a voice for the voiceless, he discovers the language that will render Benjy's feelings as a *stream-of-sensation*. In this way he conveys the incommunicable anguish of the inarticulate.

How "true" is Benjy? Readers who ask this question are often prompted to remark that it is difficult enough to get into anyone's head, let alone that of an idiot. Is not stream-of-consciousness writing a shadow-chase, since the writer in reality knows only one consciousness, his own? From birth to death we are confined within walls of private experience, sovereign and isolated, and able only to have the briefest glimpses, and at only the smallest portions, of each other's mental landscape. To ask these questions is also to recognize the courage of the artists who sought to represent in literature that which lies beyond individual experience—sought to do it armed largely with empathy and imagination. If the artist possesses imagination enough and observes closely, there is, in reality, nothing that he may not do by the process long ago described by Henry James— "the power to guess the unseen from the seen, to trace the implication of things, to judge the whole piece by the pattern, the condition of feeling life in general so completely that you are well on your way to knowing any particular corner of it." These are the gifts, said James, which constitute experience, and out of such experience the writer weaves his work.

In the old novels, those which were told as

historical narratives, we are nearly always seated face to face with the novelist; it is he who is looking out of a window and telling us the story of what he sees.[1] He offers us no choice but to listen to his story in this way; he never yields the seat at the window. When he is a fine story-teller we are prepared to accept his presence and his authority, his wisdom, his omniscience, above all, his temperament. He becomes a part of the story he tells.

In the novel of subjectivity, on the other hand, the author has left the room even before we arrive. He has placed the only seat available directly before the window and that is where we must sit. Somewhere else, beyond, below, behind, he arranges the scenery to give us an illusion that what is happening outside is happening to us. We seem to be in one of our own dreams: we become observer and actor at the same time. If we stop to remind ourselves, we may become aware that it is all an illusion artfully created for us. The degree of our par-

[1] I am borrowing an image here which I used in my book *The Psychological Novel* (New York and London, 1955).

ticipation depends on the degree of our empathy as well as our interest.

When we read this type of novel we accomplish something we can never do in our daily lives. We actually succeed in penetrating into the consciousness of another and sometimes into the inner worlds of several persons. When Virginia Woolf has made us aware of Mrs. Dalloway and her friends, not by describing them but by letting us see them as they see each other, and shown us London on a certain day through these various personages, the vision we have is no longer single: it is multiple and varied, and rich with the tones of subjective experience. And when Faulkner has taken us through the inner lives of the three Compsons, including that of the idiot, he has made us aware of the buried life of a whole family, and by the same process he has cast a new light upon the inner history of the South.

How can we speak of the novel as a dying form when it is capable of such richness and refinement? How can we say that the novel has run its course when in the three-quarters of a century since Dujardin's experiment it has shown us that it is capable of evoking a whole new side of life? The century that has produced Joyce and Proust, Woolf and Faulkner, has been admirably creative and the scope of the novel has been immeasurably widened. If there has been a lag, it lies with the reader; for to read subjective fiction one must unlearn reading habits of the past. Similarly criticism has erred in discussing the novel of subjectivity in the same terms as the conventional novel. There is much to be said about the reader's problem; Harry Levin was alluding to it when he spoke of the bond of sympathy which identifies reader and book coming "almost too close for comfort." But a discussion of this belongs to another place. What I can only add here is that in the now tolerably long history of bold and arrogant creation in our time, we must accord recognition to the precursor, to this little novel from the Symbolist workshop, with the dew sprinkled over its banalities and the fascination it offers us of reading the minor work which inaugurated a major movement.

New York University   LEON EDEL

We'll to the Woods
No More

$\mathcal{E}$VENING LIGHT of sunset, air far away, deep skies; a ferment of crowds, noises, shadows; spaces stretched out endlessly; a listless evening.

And, from the chaos of appearance, in this time of all times, this place of places, amid the illusions of things self-begotten and self-conceived, one among others, one like the others yet distinct from them, the same and yet one more, from the infinity of possible lives, I arise. So time and place come to a point; it is the Now and Here, this hour that is striking, and all around me life; the time and place, an April evening, Paris; an evening of bright sunset, a monotone of sound, white houses, foliage of shadows; a soft evening growing softer, and the joy of being oneself, of going one's way; streets, crowds and, in air far aloft, outstretched, the sky; Paris is singing all around me, and languorously composes in the mist of apprehended shapes a setting for my thought.

The hour is striking, six, the hour I waited for. Here is the house I have to enter, where I shall meet someone; the house; the hall; let's go in. Evening has come; good the air is now; something cheerful in the air. The stairs; the first steps. Supposing he has left early; he sometimes does; but I have got to tell him the story of my day. The first landing; wide, bright staircase; windows. He's a fine fellow, friend of mine; I have told him all about my love-affair. Another pleasant evening coming on. Anyway he can't make fun of me after this. I'm going to have a splendid time. Now why is the stair carpet turned up at the corner here? A grey patch on the line of upward red, on the red strip looping up from step to step. Second storey; the door on the left. *Office.* I only hope he hasn't gone; no chance of running him to earth if he has. Oh well, in that case, I'd go for a stroll down the boulevard. No time to lose; in! The outer office. Where is Lucien Chavainne? The huge room ringed with chairs. There he is, leaning over the table; overcoat and hat on; he's arranging some papers with one of the clerks; seems in a hurry. Over there the library of blue files, rows of knotted tapes. I pause on the threshold. A great time I shall have telling him all about it! Chavainne looks up; he sees me. Hullo!

— Ah, there you are! You're just in time; we clear out at six, you know. If you can wait a moment we'll go down together.

— Right!

The window is open; beyond it a grey court-yard, flooded with light; high grey walls bright in sunshine; heavenly weather. Nice the way Leah said to me: This evening, then . . . That pretty, teasing smile of hers when she spoke; reminded me of two months ago. Hullo, there's a maid at that window, looking out; now she's blushing. Why, I wonder? Ah, she's gone now.

— Ready.

Chavainne is speaking; he has taken his stick and opens the door; we go out; side by side we walk down the stairs. He speaks:

— You're wearing your bowler hat.

— Yes.

Sounded reproachful. Now why shouldn't I sport a bowler? That's the sort of chap he is, thinks that trifles like that count if one wants to look smart. The concierge's den; there's never anyone there; rum sort of house this is. Surely Chavainne will come a little way with me. But he's a tiresome fellow, always wants to go straight home. In the street now; a carriage waiting at the entrance; shopfronts flashing sunlight; in front the Tour Saint-Jacques; we are going towards the Châtelet.

— How is your love-affair getting on?

He wants to know; I'll tell him.

—Much as before.

We are walking side by side.

— Have you just come from her place?

— Yes, I went to see her. We passed a couple of hours talking, singing, playing the piano. She said I was to meet her to-night at the stage-door.

And how charmingly she said it!

— Really!

— And you, old fellow — what's the latest?

— Oh, nothing . . .

Silence. Fascinating she is! Got quite upset because she broke down in one of the verses; as a matter of fact I was playing out of time, but I didn't tell her; must be more careful when I'm accompanying her again to-night.

— You know, she only comes on now in the first act. I shall meet her at the Nouveautés Theatre at about nine; we'll go for a drive, towards the Bois, I expect; perfect weather, isn't it? Then I'll see her home.

— And you'll try to stay the night with her?

— No.

The last thing in the world I'd do. Will Chavainne never understand my ideas on the subject?

— What a queer chap you are, he says, with your Platonic love!

Queer . . . Platonic . . .

— Well that's the way I feel about it; I'd rather take a line of my own than follow the herd.

— All very fine, my dear fellow, but do you realise the kind of girl she is?

— Certainly. An actress in a small theatre.

And that's just why I choose to behave as I am doing.

— You imagine she will be touched?

Now he's grinning; impossible he is. No, my friend, she is not that sort of girl at all. And even if she were . . . The Rue de Rivoli; must cross now; mind the traffic; what a crowd! Six o'clock; the rush hour, especially in this part of Paris; a tram honking; look out!

— Seems to me there's more room on the right of the road.

We walk along the pavement, side by side. Chavainne speaks.

— The pleasure you get out of it isn't worth the racket. Why, it's three months since you came to know this girl and . . .

— I've been seeing her for three months, yes. But, as you're aware, I've known her for over four.

— Exactly. You have been ruining yourself for four months, and all for nothing.

— Excuse me, old fellow, but you're talking nonsense.

— Before you'd said a single word to her you gave her, through her maid, five hundred francs.

Five hundred? No, three. Ah, of course, I told Chavainne it was five hundred.

— If you imagine, he continues, that throwing money about in that way will induce a professional actress to give something in return . . . Change your tactics, my friend, or you'll never get anything.

Confound him and his casuistry! Can't he realize that, if I get nothing in return, it is precisely because I don't want to get anything? I'm a fool to discuss such things with him. Better change the subject.

— I suppose I'm stupid enough to choose to behave like this instead of wasting my nights with casual pick-ups.

One in the eye for you! Now he's silent. A good fellow is Lucien Chavainne, no doubt, but no sentiment, not an atom of it. That's the thing: to love, to treat one's love with respect, to take it seriously, to be in love with love! It's warm out walking to-day; I unbutton my overcoat; let's see, I think I'll wear my tail coat this evening when I go out with Leah; better than this lounge suit; might wear my silk hat too; Chavainne is right in a way; one can't possibly wear a bowler with a long coat. Leah never mentions my clothes; notices them all the same, I expect. Chavainne:

— I'm going to the Comédie Française to-night.

— What's the show?

— *Ruy Blas.*

— You're really going to see that?

— Why not?

Not worth answering. The idea of going to see *Ruy Blas* in 1887! He continues:

— I have never seen the play and, I admit, I'm curious to find out what it's like.

— What an old romantic you are!

— You call me a romantic?

— Why not?

— Why, it's you are a romantic, a regular double-dyed romantic! How about this love-affair of yours? . . . Just because you happened to see some show or other at the Nouveautés . . .

Lovely she was that night!

— All this winter, old chap, you've been working yourself up and now you're absolutely crazy over her. No but really . . . ! And do you remember how, when we were leaving the

theatre, it was I who had a look at the poster
and told you the lady's name? From that moment
you began to get keen on her, and now you're
wallowing in Platonic love!

Well-dressed that fellow passing now, a rose
in his buttonhole; yes, I'd better have a flower in
mine to-night; I might bring something for Leah
too. Chavainne has stopped talking; stupid chap
he is! Of course, I'll admit, my love for Leah is
something out of the usual run; and so much the
better. A street; Rue de Marengo; the Louvre
Stores; a dense file of carriages. Chavainne:

— I'll have to leave you at the Palais-Royal.

What a bore he is! Always giving one the slip
like that! We are under the arcade now; walking past the shop windows; in the crowd.
Better walk on the road. No, too many carriages.
Bit of a crush here, but it can't be helped. A
woman in front; tall, slim, heavily scented;
shapely figure she has, flashing red hair; wonder
what her face is like; handsome, probably.
Chavainne is speaking.

— Come with me to-night to the theatre.
After, we can go for a stroll somewhere.

— I told you I had an appointment.

13

That red-haired girl is stopping before a shop window; bold features she has, to match her hair; looks pretty wideawake; painted eyes; a big white bow at her throat; looking our way now, at me; what alluring eyes! Now we're quite close to her. Awfully fetching girl.

— Let's slow down a bit.

— Your appointment doesn't interfere; as you've decided not to stay at Mademoiselle d'Arsay's place, you can turn up for the last act or meet me outside or anywhere you like, and we can go for a midnight stroll together.

Is he chaffing me?

— And you can tell me all about your conversation with Mademoiselle d'Arsay.

Yes, I suppose it could be managed after I leave her.

— Doesn't that suit you? What do you do with yourself after you leave your flame?

— Really, where are your wits, my dear fellow?

Now we are silent; I think he is smiling; of all the fools — ! The Palais-Royal square. Where's that red-haired girl got to? Vanished; no luck. Chavainne:

— What are you looking for?

— Oh nothing.

Vanished. That's what you've done for me, my dear sir.

— I'll just step across to the Théâtre-Français to see what time the show begins.

Still harping on his show! Wait. I'd like to tell him before he goes all about this afternoon. The little drawing-room in a half-light filtered through the yellow curtains; Leah in a kind mood; she wore that white satin peignoir, falling in wide silky folds round her slender body; behind the big white collar her throat, a pink triangle; smiling she came towards me; her pale face set in fair tendrils of her hair, gold rippling upon her shoulders; all daintiness she is, my darling girl, and so young, nineteen, twenty perhaps; she owns to eighteen; ah, she's an exquisite creature.

Past the calm frontage of the Palais-Royal, past the Palais-Royal we go. She held out her hand to me; I kissed her forehead; very chastely; she leant against my shoulder and for an instant we stayed like that, without moving, and across the satin my hands clasped the soft warmth of her. Oh how I love her, my lovedear! And to think that all these people passing by have no idea of such happiness as mine, that it means nothing to all these people hurrying beside me, indifferent, the crowd!

— Here's a poster. It begins at eight. Sure you can't come?

— Impossible.

— Au revoir, then; I must be getting home.

— Au revoir. Hope you have a good time.

Nice fellow he is . . . Hope you enjoy your dinners, gentlemen . . . Supposing now that girl fancied me, became my mistress. . . . Ah, I have been with her, the angel of my world! . . Chavainne's voice.

— And I hope you have a good time, too. But, mind, don't do anything rash.

— No fear.

— You'll let me know what happens?

— Yes. *Au revoir.*

We shake hands. He turns back. *Au revoir.* I'll go up the Avenue de l'Opéra; might dine at the café at the corner of the Avenue and the Rue des Petits-Champs; I shall have plenty of time to get back to my place by nine. The post-office;

really must write to my people; letter's overdue; oh, I'll write to-morrow; to-morrow there's that law lecture; with only three courses of lectures to attend, I can't decently cut it, no. So Chavainne is going to the Théâtre Français to-night. Yes, a good fellow, but a bit too sophisticated, one can't feel at ease with him or talk freely; quick in the uptake; well-groomed, too, good taste he has; it's a pleasure to be with him; next time I must explain my reasons for behaving as I do; pity I didn't tell him more about this afternoon; he might perhaps have guessed something of the peculiar charm of a love like mine; but no, such things mean nothing to him; love which is contented by mere friendship; a woman one loves and venerates. It is two months now since the first, the only time she gave herself to me; that was at the beginning, no, the middle of February. They are lighting the gaslamps in the Avenue; night is coming. How will she be dressed when we come back? Her blue cashmere gown, I expect, a long plait of hair hanging down her back; one'd take her for a little schoolgirl, a bread and butter miss; some evenings she's so gay, laughing all the time; comic air of dignity she had that day in her black dress; another time she'd just come from her bath, all pink and white, hair brushed flat. If only I could do more for her! Mother is sure to send me some cash for Easter, that will help things out. The corner of the Rue des Petits-Champs; lights on in the café already; why, all the shops in the Avenue are lit up; curious how quickly it gets dark! *Café Oriental, Restaurant.* Duval's eating-house on the other side; supposing I went there to economize a bit? Sound idea that, to economize. No, the café's far better really and there's not much difference in price; Duval's, too, is quite a decent place, not so comfortable, but quite decent; never mind, here's for the café and damn the expense! I see the lights inside, red and gold reflected; the street in shadow; vapour on the windows. *Dinners, three francs . . . Beer, thirty centimes.* Leah would never consent to dine here. In. Just one twirl to the tips of my moustache now; that's got it.

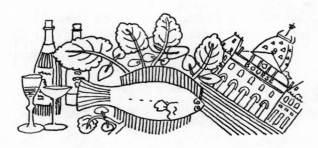

ℛED AND GOLD, a glare of light,
the café; flashing mirrors; a white-aproned
waiter; pillars hung with hats and overcoats.
Anyone here I know? Those people are watching
me come in; a thin chap with long whiskers,
looks the regular heavy father. All the tables
taken, where shall I sit? An empty place down
there, capital, my usual table; why shouldn't a
fellow have his favourite table? Nothing for
Leah to laugh at in that.

— Yes, sir?

The waiter. The table. My hat on the peg.
Take gloves off; drop them casually on the table,
beside the plate; or shall I in my overcoat pocket?
No, on the table; it's trifles like that show a
fellow's style. Hang up my coat now; sit down;
that's better; really fagged I was. Yes, I'll put

my gloves in the overcoat pocket after all. Red and gold it is, with a glare of lights, those flashing mirrors; what? The café, of course, the café where I'm sitting. Lord, how fagged I was! The waiter.

— Clear soup, Saint-Germain, bisque . . .

— Clear.

— To follow, sir?

— Let's see the menu.

— And the wine, red or white?

— Red, please.

The menu. Let's see; fish, sole . . . yes, a sole. *Entrées*, mutton cutlets . . . no. Chicken . . . yes.

— Sole. Then some chicken, with watercress.

— Yes, sir. Sole, chicken and cress.

So I'm going to dine, and a very good idea too. Now that's a pretty woman over there; neither fair nor dark; a high-stepper, by gad; tallish, probably; must be the wife of that bald man with his back to me; more likely his mistress; somehow she hasn't just the married air; quite a pretty girl, really. She might look this way; almost exactly opposite me she is; what shall I?

Oh, what's the good? There, she's spotted me. Really a pretty woman, and the man looks a bore; a pity I can only see his back; I'd like to have a look at his face too; lawyer, I should say, a family solicitor up from the country. Absurd I am! How about the soup? The glass in front reflects the gilded frame; the gilded frame behind me of course; those arabesques in bright vermilion, all scarlet flashes; but the light is pale yellow; walls, napery, mirrors, wineglasses, all yellowed by the gaslight. It's comfortable here, well-appointed place. Here's the soup, piping hot; waiter might splash some, better keep an eye on him. All's well; let's begin. Too hot, this soup; wait, try again. Not half bad. I lunched a bit too late, no appetite left. All the same I must eat some dinner. Soup finished. That woman looked this way again; expressive eyes she has and the man with her seems a dull bird; I might get to know her by some fluke; queerer things happen; why not? If I keep on looking at her, it might lead to something; but they've reached the joint already; never mind, if I choose I can catch them up at the post. Where's that waiter gone to? Slow as a funeral they are,

these restaurant dinners; I might fix up to have my meals at home; the concierge could do the cooking, and it would be cheaper too. He'd make a mess of it, for a certainty. I'm a fool; deadly dull it would be, and how about the days when I don't come back? At least in a restaurant one isn't bored. What's that waiter up to? Coming now with the sole. Funny things soles. About four mouthfuls in this one and there are others would make a meal for ten people; of course they eke it out with sauce. Let's start on it anyhow. A shrimp-and-mussel sauce would be a distinct improvement. That time we went shrimping at the seaside; a rotten catch, boring performance it was and my feet were sopping, though I was wearing those stout tan shoes I bought near the Bourse. What an endless business it is picking away at a fish; I seem to make no headway! I must owe a hundred francs, more, to my bootmaker. I might try to learn up about stocks and shares at the Bourse; that would be a sound idea. I could never make out what they mean by speculating for a fall; how on earth can one make money over shares that go down? Suppose I put a hundred thousand francs in

Panamas and they go down; then I sell, yes, and I must buy in again at the next rise; no, dash it, I should sell. That fat old solicitor over there might oblige with an explanation. Perhaps he's not a lawyer at all. Confound these bones! All bones this sole is; but the flavour's good. There, that's enough, leave the rest. I lean back now; more people coming in; all men; that fellow looks ill at ease; an odd light-coloured overcoat he has; that shade went out of fashion years ago. I've left a tempting morsel of my sole; no, I won't take it now, it would look silly. That little white morsel would taste fine, with all the lines the bones have made on it. Oh, well, let it go. Better clean my hands on the napkin, rough feel it has, new perhaps. That solicitor's wife has just turned; it looked almost as if she made a sign to me; what striking eyes! How can I get to speak to her? Now she has stopped looking. Shall I send a note? No, that might land me with a snub; wait, though . . . I might show her the note and, if she wanted, she could manage somehow or other to take it; in any case I might as well have the note ready. But, there, I've got to go home and change and be at the theatre

25

before nine; infernal nuisance all these compli-
cations are.

— Finished, sir?

— Yes. You can bring the chicken.

— Very good, sir.

A glass of wine. The places opposite me are
empty; leather upholstery between them and
the mirror. Yes, I must try my luck with a note.
My cardcase; a card with my address on it; that's
the correct thing; my pocket-pencil, right. What
shall I say? An appointment for to-morrow.
Better give her the choice of where. If that solicitor, stout fellow, knew what I was up to! I
write: *To-morrow at two o'clock in the reading room
at.* At one of the big shops; the *Louvre;* — *at the
Louvre.* Not quite high-life, perhaps, but very
handy; can't imagine any better place. That's it.
At two o'clock at the Louvre. I mustn't pin her
down as to time; better say from two to three,
anyhow. Yes, I change *at* to *from,* and add *till
three.* Next: *I shall . . . I shall look out for you;* no,
I shall be looking out for you. Easy now; let's see.
*To-morrow from two o'clock till three in the reading-
room at the Louvre I shall be . . .* Hopelessly
clumsy. Now how shall I put it? Wait. Yes: At

two o'clock in the reading-room and so on *till three
I shall be* . . . Let's say till four o'clock; yes, I
can bring a book, that book by what's-his-name,
that journalist chap. Can't imagine why I
bought it the other evening; still, as I've got it,
I may as well find out what it's about. I'll
choose a seat there and wait for her in comfort;
but how about the draughts? Oh, they're nothing
much; no, there aren't any draughts. Now I
really must get the note finished. *I shall be looking
out for you* . . . wait; I have to put back *at* instead of *from*; right. *To-morrow at two* . . . No,
I say, my card will be covered with corrections,
hideous, illegible. It's absurd; and I'll catch a
cold in that rotten reading-room, full of draughts
as it is, and, in any case, she will refuse to accept
my note. There, I tear it up; in two pieces; tear
across; four pieces; again; that makes eight.
Again; no, imposs. It won't do to drop these
bits of card on the floor; someone might pick
them up; better try chewing them. Ugh! Horrible
taste. Drop them then; there's no fear of anyone
reading. That woman is laughing; but I'm sure
she hasn't looked this way once in the last few
minutes; now she's looking, saying something to

27

the man. What a pretty girl she is, yes, really pretty! This chewed paper tastes awful; have a drink to take it away; that's better. Let's consult the menu; spring peas, asparagus, no; ices, coffee ice, yes. I'm not a bit hungry really. Dessert, cheese, meringues, apples. The waiter is bringing the chicken. It looks appetizing.

— I will take a coffee ice, and after — have you any camembert?

— Yes, sir.

— Camembert, please.

Now for the chicken; a wing this time; not so tough; some bread; not a bad bird at all; this is a good place to dine; next time Leah and I dine together at her flat I'll order the dinner at that place in Rue Favert; it's cheaper there than the smart restaurants, and better. The wine here is nothing special; you have to go to a first class place to get proper wine. Wine, cards — wine, cards and women — so they say; but what has wine got to do with cards or cards with women? Of course there's fellows have to be a bit on before they can make love, but where do the cards come in? Quite a decent chicken and the watercress deuced good. Ah, pleasant sensation

this towards the end of a good meal! Where do
the cards come in? . . . Wine, cards . . . wine,
cards and women. Woman, charming woman, so
dear to M. Scribe. No, that's not in *Le Chalet*
but in *Robert-le-Diable*; devil take it! that's Scribe
too. The three together always, a triple passion
. . . *Vive le vin, l'amour et le tabac. Voilà, voilà, le
refrain du bivouac.* Tobacco, too, of course; I was
forgetting it. How should one pronounce them,
taba-c and *bivoua-c* or *taba* and *bivoua*? Mendès, in
the Boulevard des Capucines used to pronounce
dompter, dom-p-ter; dom-ter is right, of course.
L'amour et le tabac . . . *le refrain du bivouac* . . .
The solicitor and his wife are going. How absurd,
silly, idiotic of me to let them slip off like that!
— Waiter!

I'll pay at once and catch them up. At the
door now.
— Waiter!

Not a sign of him; it's rotten luck; prize idiot
I am missing a chance like that; these things only
happen once; exceptionally charming she was.
She didn't look my way when she got up; only
natural, after all. Well, they're off. A marvellous
adventure it might have been; I could have

29

followed her, found out where she was going; something'd have come of it, for a certainty. Which way did she go, I wonder? They turned to the right, must have gone up the Avenue de l'Opéra. Is there an opera on to-night? Yes, of course, it's a Monday. One of these evenings I must take darling little Leah to the opera; she'll love it.

— Yes, sir?

The waiter. What does he want? Did I call? Of course I did.

— I am rather in a hurry, you see . . .

— Certainly, sir.

Waiter looks as if he were laughing at me up his sleeve. Well, I suppose I am a bit ridiculous. Why bother about other women? Quite well off as I am, thank you. Why want another? It's so tiring all this running after women. More people going out. Interminable this dinner is. The ice, bravo, let's sample it; slowly; it's delicious; cool, coffee-flavoured, cool flavour on tongue and palate. One can't get that sort of thing at home. He must have felt tired that fellow who took his son to watch the people eating ices at Tortoni's. Tortoni's; I've never tried it; never set foot inside. *Just try it, just try it; goes to that tune in the Dame Blanche; just try it.* Ice finished now; a pity. The cheese is here, I never saw him bring it. Must drink some water first. Well, in a fortnight or so I shall get away from Paris; if it's fine all the family will be staying at Quevilly; too cold in April to go to the country. Must give the cheese a miss; no appetite left. What a bore it is always dining at a restaurant, with no one to talk to, not a woman to look at; not a woman for a week; nothing but men, the would-be smart variety, too hard up to go to a better place; on the rocks, so they come here; solicitors up from the country who fancy they are at Bignon's. Three francs, and ten sous for the tip; and so good-night. I get up; put on my overcoat; the waiter is pretending to help; thanks; my hat, gloves, ah yes, in the pocket; out of here. That table over there, by the pillar, would have suited me better; people drinking beer; the big doors now, massive, mirrored; a waiter opens; good-night; brr, it's cold; better button my coat; after that heat inside it's the contrast; he is shutting the door; *Beer, thirty centimes . . . Dinners, three francs.*

31

THE STREET is dark; but it's only
half past seven; I'll go home; I shall have heaps
of time to get to the Nouveautés by nine. The
Avenue isn't quite so dark as it seemed, after
all; not a cloud in the sky; a sheen on the pavement, light from the street-lamps; three gasjets
per lamp; not many people about; the Opéra up
there, with its vestibule a blaze of lights; I am
taking the right hand side of the Avenue, going
towards the Opéra. There, I've forgotten to
put on my gloves; doesn't matter, I shall be home
in no time and anyhow there's not a soul about
now. I shall be home in: let's see . . . five
minutes to the Opéra; five to the Rue Auber,
the Boulevard Haussmann about the same; five
more, that makes, ten, fifteen, twenty minutes.
I shall dress; I can leave at half past eight, say

eight thirty-five. Fine and dry it is; just the weather for an after-dinner stroll; there never are many people in the Avenue at this time of the evening. Leah gets out of the theatre at nine, between nine and a quarter past. What shall we do? A drive round, yes, we can drive along the boulevard to the Champs-Elysées, as far as the Rond-Point; no, better go up to the Arc de Triomphe, and we can come back to her place along the outer boulevards; it's such lovely weather; of course she'll let me hold her hand; I expect she will be wearing that black cash-mere dress; must take care we don't get back too late; it's a certainty she'll ask me in for a bit; then I shall watch that saucy little devil's smile of hers and slowly, slowly, she will set about her evening toilette. — Sit down in the arm-chair now, like a good boy, she will say, making one of those ceremonious gestures of hers, and I shall reply in the same tone: — Certainly, Mademoiselle! I shall sit in that armchair, up-holstered in blue velvet with a big band of embroidery round it; in that chair she once sat on my knee, a fortnight ago it was; I shall sit in the low chair near her, facing the wardrobe

33

mirror; she will stand in front of it, put her hat
on the plush table and settle her hair with little
pats, first one side, then the other, pausing now
and then, preening herself, back view, front
view, with little pats, looking round at me,
laughing, making faces at me, like a naughty
child she is, a naughty, delightful child! In her
black skirt and black cashmere blouse; not big,
not small, though she looks small, no, not really
small; young, I mean, like a little girl; delight-
fully plump, too; under her tiny waist, wide
rounded hips with a graceful downward curve,
all softness; her proud little breast, fine the way
it can flutter on great occasions; her mischievous
child's face, hair pale gold, big eyes; too, too
lovely! My little Leah, how I adore her! Yes, I
must love her with pure devotion, the best kind
of love and not like other fellows do. When we
get back it will be ten at the earliest. There's the
pneumatic clock; seven thirty-five. The Opéra.
The terrace of the Café de la Paix is packed; no
one there I know; the Opéra; Rue Auber; M.
Vaudier's house; it must be two months since I
last dined at his place, perhaps he's away; he's
tremendously rich, it's devilish fine to have a

34

fortune like that; how much, I wonder? A million a year, someone said; that means a capital of twenty millions at least; almost a hundred thousand francs a month; wait; a million divided by twelve, let's say a hundred divided by twelve . . . nought, twelve into . . . better put it at ninety-six, nine hundred and sixty thousand francs; ninety-six divided by twelve is eight, eighty; eighty thousand francs a month. Oh, if only Leah could have a grand house of her own; a sweet child she is; if I had all that money; let's pretend; suppose I had come into a fortune; build castles in the air, an excellent idea; well, the lawyer has handed me the scrip; I'd get cash, gold and notes, right away, a hundred thousand francs; I'd go to see Leah just as usual, as if nothing had happened, and say to her suddenly, like that: — Leah, will you let's go away at once; I'm running away with you; I kidnap you, you kidnap me . . . Steady now, no nonsense! I might say, for instance: — Will you come away with me? She wouldn't believe her ears. Quite impossible, she would say. — Why? . . . Then she'd explain how it was impossible for her to give up her career and so on. I'd reply in a

natural tone of voice, oh quite casually: — Don't
you worry about that, I've had a stroke of luck;
I can look after you now. If you have any debts,
any liabilities, just let me fix them up so that
you can get away at once . . . That's all right
. . . Just you let me fix things up for you. Then
I'd lay ten thousand francs on a table or something and add: — If you need more just tell me
. . . Ten thousand francs, well perhaps five; no,
for a start ten thousand would be better; anyhow, the amount wouldn't worry me. Twenty
thousand? No, that would be overdoing it; ten
thousand, that's exactly right. And wouldn't
she be knocked over, and overjoyed all at once!
— Now, I'd ask, what about starting off right
away? — What, start right away? — Yes, I
mean it, give all this up, leave everything behind;
you'll get it all back a hundred times over; just
you and I together, let's clear out, travel together, far away. Then I'd take her in my arms
and kiss her hair; I'd carry her down; and softly,
yes softly she'd whisper Yes; like in Gauthier's
Fortunio; but Fortunio set light to the curtains
and carried her off naked; well, with a million a
year I could afford to be a bit eccentric too. The

Eden Theatre; a flare of gaslamps, electric light as well; programme-sellers; street-urchin opening a cab door; now why does one need a street-urchin to open the door of one's cab? Down there the Printemps; not a soul in sight; usually there are a lot of afterdusks here, and a deuced nuisance they are, accosting one; none about to-night, however; gloomy the street is. Let's come back to the point. I am going to kill time working out what I'd do if I suddenly got rich; yes, let's work it all out as I walk home. So then . . . my ship's come home; what ship? That's a detail. I'm rich and there's an end of it. Very well, I have come into a fortune this very evening and my pockets are full of money. I've no wish to run a large establishment; just a bachelor flat would do, and a house of her own for Leah; why, I might keep on my fourth-floor digs in the Rue du Général Foy; well, something of the sort, but a bit smarter. I could live at my own place like a bachelor with an income of, say, thirty thousand francs, and spend a million a year on my mistress; a little ground-floor flat would suit, in the Parc Monceau district, obviously; five or six rooms; a carriage-entrance, of course; then

two steps; the door, a hall, in front a little drawing-room, dining-room and smoking-room; behind, kitchen, privies, a bedroom with a big
dressing-room; the bedroom opening on a bit of a
garden. The hall would need to be pretty large;
I'd have a sort of conservatory there all along the
front . . . no, that wouldn't do, better if it
stopped short at the dining-room; between dining-room and bedroom a second hall, separated
from the other by a door, no, a curtain would
be better — come in handy if I should want
to smuggle in a girl or two! Furniture? No
showy vulgar stuff; a style all my own; my ideal
always was a white bedroom with no other
furniture in it; just a square bed in the middle of
the room; a brass bedstead, no upholstery, brass
and white go together; walls draped with satin,
cashmere, white silk and so forth; the ceiling too;
white rugs on the floor, polar-bear skins obviously indicated. Above all, no furniture; my
wardrobes in the dressing-room; only divans in
the bedroom . . . Hullo! Where have we got to?
Ah yes, coming into the Boulevard Haussmann.
The drawing-room door on the left; a window
on the right; in front the dressing-room door;

bed opposite; where the fireplace? In front, yes, in place of the dressing-room door. How about the door then? Oh, in the corner somewhere. Might do without the fireplace, or have it in the corner; in the corner, too, or perhaps in the middle of the ceiling one of those nightlamp affairs in alabaster, rather like the one in Leah's bedroom. The lavatory in marble, obviously. Now should the hall be in marble too, I wonder? Shrubs all along the wall. How about the lighting in the hall? Skylights are always such dingy things. And I'd want to have the house in a quiet street. That would be the thing — a few yards of garden between the house and the street; a low wall, plain iron gate; a little garden with one or two lilac-bushes, some shrubs too, any old kind of shrub. How wide? A yard and a half or two yards. Ass I am. Three to five yards. It really depends on whether there is a door leading to the garden; pretty useless it would be; not unpleasant, though, provided it opened from the dining-room; might come in very handy sometimes; that's it, three to six yards of garden. Let's measure. Three yards, three strides. One, two, three. That's it. When I chose to dine at home, the servant would fix it up with Chevet or some other place; the simple life, there's nothing to touch it; in any case I'd spend most of my time at Leah's place; now and then I'd invite her to my bachelor digs, just for an escapade; thrilling it would be to make love in our white room amongst the polar-bear skins. So this very evening we would be running away, she and I; in two hours I'd be at her place with twenty-five thousand francs in my pocket; I'd turn up just as usual. Ah, but of course I'm not going to her house; I shall meet her at the theatre; well, it's all the same.

— Good evening, Monsieur.

Hullo! A professional. If I seem to be looking at her she'll hang on to me.

— Monsieur . . .

A reek of patchouli. Whew! Get clear of that. Ah Leah, my own dear girl, dear little girl I love, how happy you would be, the bad times all over and done with, and how we would love each other when I told you I had become rich, and all for you, and we could leave Paris together, this very evening! Where would we go? To my rooms first of all, then to-morrow we'd start on our travels; no, we'd have to do our

shopping to-morrow; we could start the next
day; till then together at my place. There I'd
be as usual at the theatre, at nine or thereabouts,
waiting for her. Now she comes out; I greet her.
— Good evening, Mademoiselle! On the left
there, in that side street, that tall young man,
thin, with a top hat and short black overcoat;
who is it? Why, it's Paul Hénart! Coming this
way. Hénart, immaculate as usual, with his slim
Malacca cane; he has seen me; he's waving.
— Evening.
— Evening. Homeward bound?
— Yes. How are you? Coming my way?
— Yes. I'll go with you as far as Saint-
Augustin's.
— Capital! Any news?
— Nothing. Nothing, so far.
It's good to see Hénart again; old friend, cap-
ital fellow, fine chap he is. Perfect manners too,
one of the best, the sort one can trust, and cheery
as they're made. We walk along the boule-
vard. Handsome into the bargain; never puts on
airs though. Where's he going? Might ask.
— This doesn't take you to your place.
— No, I am going to the Rue de Courcelles.

I see; that old story about a marriage. Still at it, is he?

— Rue de Courcelles? You're going to see that lady whose daughter —

— That's it.

— You told me something about it once — ages ago that was. How are things going?

— We'll be getting married soon.

— Really?

— Yes, really. Are you surprised?

— No.

Marriage; to marry the woman one loves; to be able to marry the woman one loves; to possess her. So these things really happen: marriage, being together, a life in common.

— No, I reply, I'm not surprised. But how did you bring it off so quickly?

Going to get married! What a fellow he is with his precious love-affair, his marriage; you'd think these things never happened to anyone else in the world!

— What do you expect me to do? he replies. I am in love with a girl who loves me and I'm going to marry her.

— And you're pleased about it.

— Very pleased.

— Lucky dog!

— I have found a woman worth loving, who knows how to love.

Really he seems to think he's the only fellow on earth who loves and is loved. Still, I seem to remember . . .

— My dear Hénart, if my memory serves me, you once let fall two or three remarks which gave me the idea it was quite by accident that you came across this girl . . .

— By accident, yes. I saw her one day, for the first time, in a public garden with two other girls; I was strolling casually past; she was there — there was something so . . . so innocent, so pure about her! That was six months ago. I found out where she lived, then her name and who she was. That's how it happened.

Exactly . . . that's how it happened. He admits it. In a public garden; three girls; I choose a seat in front; with my eyeglass in my eye . . . And I followed her home. Exactly!

— And when a mathematician falls in love, of course, it's all up with him. Did you speak to her?

— Not at once. She noticed me, so she told me later. I learned that she was living with her mother. You can guess the rest.

— You wrote to her?

— No. A friend of a friend of mine introduced me to them.

By procuration. Exactly!

— I found in her a girl capable of sincere feeling, a deep-hearted, sensible girl, who could look me in the face — a true woman, in fact. I visited her mother, nice woman she is too, and she understood, she trusted me, that wonderful, splendid mother of hers. It sounds like a story by Madame de Ségur, doesn't it? The old lady passes her evenings knitting — like in old-fashioned novels — or plays the piano; Elise and I talk to each other.

Sweet simplicity!

— And that's been going on for six months?

— Five or six. The evening we got engaged she was all in white, sitting in an armchair; I had a low chair beside her; it was in a corner of the drawing-room; her mother persists in trying to read difficult music at sight, Jansen and so on.

Elise, without moving, whispered to me, so softly that her lips did not seem to move, one almost imagined that someone else, not she, was speaking; this is what she said: — The first evening you came here I would have said Yes if I'd had the courage. And then she said to me: — Yes, dear, I'll marry you. Those were the words. You picture the scene? Then her mother turned and looked at us. — Very well, young people, she said; and married you shall be. Don't mind me! And then she burst out laughing, so lightheartedly, with such glee, that . . . and so forth and so on!

The moral of the story, evidently.

— Capital, old chap, capital! I've greatly enjoyed hearing your love story. So you'll be married soon?

— This summer, I hope.

— Has she money of her own?

— Her mother has a competence; as for me, since I've had my job in the city, I've been doing pretty well.

— Capital, capital! She is twenty, I think you said, and you're twenty-seven?

— She has given some meaning to my life, something to live for. I shall be her husband and — I am utterly happy.

Utterly happy, her husband, utterly happy! Paul and I are walking together along the streets; before us stretches the Boulevard Malesherbes; trees, lights, deserted streets, a pale breeze. How I long to be away, down there in the country, at my father's house, out in the fields at night, walking alone, all, all alone! Ah, good it is in the country at night walking with a stick, forward and forward, on and on, dreaming all sorts of things; silently, in the vast lonely countryside, swinging along the deep roads; ah good it is, good! Paul and I are walking side by side . . .

— You're a lucky fellow, Hénart.

— I wish you the same sort of luck. I shall be seeing her in a few minutes; she's expecting me, but she doesn't show her eagerness for fear her mother should make fun of her. Here we are at Saint-Augustin's. You're going up the Avenue Portalis?

— Yes. I have to go home.

— Nothing worrying you? Quite the contrary, I suppose.

— Oh, no, nothing to speak about. Good-night, Paul.

— Good-night.

— Come and see me one day.

— One morning I'll drop in and catch you in bed — if it wouldn't be disturbing you.

— Not a bit, old boy.

— Good-night.

— Good-night.

We separate. He is going that way. Lucky chap, oh lucky chap! He has found the real thing, a love requited. And he imagines that I go with women! Requited love! He thinks he is happy, therefore he is happy; happier, perhaps, than anyone has ever been. Supposing he were the only man to know what love really is; he certainly thinks so. And yet, and yet . . . Quaint mentality he must have to swallow all that stuff, and on such evidence! Rue de Courcelles, Elise and her mother; and what is she, devil take it? A girl whom he picked up by mere chance, the sort of girl who sits about in a park with two other girls, a girl he followed, who accepted letters from him, at whose house he has been playing the simpleton; why, she'd have said Yes at once if he'd dared to propose! And that mother, too; a widow, I suppose, with small means of her own, an officer's widow, who pretends to be reading Jansen at sight; love's old sweet song; I will be your wife . . . and why not start in at once, dear boy; there's the bedroom! Wonder what you'd have said to that, Mr Civil Engineer. They played their cards well, those two women. And that ass who is deluded into thinking, who actually thinks, has the nerve to think he is in love; who doesn't see he is fooling himself or guess that in two months he will be sick of her, and goes and ties himself up . . .! That's not the way of real love; it doesn't begin like that, it's not born in that way. No, when one really falls in love, it's not in the Parc Monceau, one fine day when a fellow's taking the air, running after little shop-girls or widows' daughters, playing the rôle of Paris to a trio of Park beauties . . . My door, home at last . . . Love, the real thing? Leave that to me, my friend, that's *my* affair; holy Paul, I should say so!

Sir!

Someone calling; it's the concierge, with a letter.

— That maid who has been coming here lately brought this letter for you, sir. Urgent, she said.

Must be from Leah.

— Here . . . Thanks.

Dear Boy

Don't come to the theatre to meet me this evening. Come straight to my place about ten. I shall be expecting you.

Leah.

Confound her! Why can't she stick to her arrangements? One never knows where one is with her; first one plan and then another; it's the same story every time we are to meet. Now why doesn't she want me to meet her at the theatre? Doesn't want to be seen with me, perhaps; some other fellow in tow. Of course she may have to stay on late at the theatre; it might be some reason like that. What's this, second or third floor? The gasjet, must be the second then. Maddening girl she is, still it's as well she warned me in time; but fancy sending her maid at seven, why, I mightn't have come home, absurd I call it! And if I'd missed her note and turned up at the theatre she'd have made no end of a scene; no, she'll be afraid of running into me and leave by another door; those theatres always have dozens of exits. And a fine fool I'd have looked! But of course she knew I was bound to look in here on my way. Anyhow . . . Here's my door; I open it; darkness; matches in their place; I strike one; careful now . . . the sitting-room door; I enter; the mantelpiece, candlestick there; I light it; spent match in the ashtray; that's right; the table; no letters, yes, a visiting card, corner turned down; who can it be? *Jules de Rivare.* Now that's bad luck; he's such a good sort; we took our philosophy schools together; what a sensible chap he was! So he came to-day and that concierge never told me. Old de Rivare's back in Paris, with his black moustache and air of a cavalry officer; there's another fellow for you with perfect manners. Oh, he'll look me up again, but it was silly of him not to say where he is staying. Wait; at the back of his card, never thought of looking, there's something written. *Come to lunch with me to-morrow, eleven, Hotel Byron, Rue Laffite.* I'll go, rather! But there's that law lecture on at two; well, if I must cut it, I must. He must be well off, old de Rivare; comes of a good county family... now does he, I'm not so sure? Well, I'd better be getting dressed ready to go to Leah's; I have over an hour and a half, heaps of time for it. My hat and coat on a chair; I enter the bedroom; the two double candlesticks with their storks' necks branching up; light them; it's done. My room; on the left there my bed, white in its bamboo frame; the panel of old tapestry hanging above it; a red pattern, quiet-toned, subdued, with vague blue-violet patches on a shadowy background of deep reds and blues, all faded tints; I really must get a new mat for the dressing-room; can order one at the Bon Marché; no, there's a better choice in the Avenue de l'Opéra. Must dress now; but what's the use of changing? I shan't be able to stay on at Leah's; I shall have to come back here. Still, after all, one never knows the turn things will take; anything might happen, some lucky coincidence. Ah, when will that day come, the day that gives her to me? Anyhow, yes, I'll change; ample time I have and to spare; twenty minutes will take me to her place so there's no need to hurry. Delightful the air is to-night, so warm and languid, like a promise of happiness to come. We'll talk in the carriage, just the two of us together, driving through shadowed streets, under the clear sky, in warm languid air, lovers' weather; what a perfect evening it is! Shall I open the window? Yes, wide. Pale darkness of the night; darkness all glimmering with the earliest stars; vague half-shadows; a cloudless night. Behind me is the room, candlelight, the heavier air of rooms, moist air of stuffy indoors. I lean on the balcony, bending over the emptiness of space; I take deep breaths of the evening air, vaguely conscious of that loveliness outside, the shadowed, soft, forlorn remoteness of the air, all this night's beauty;

a grey-black sky, here and there suffused with blue, and tiny stars, like tremulous drops of water, watery stars; all around, the misty paleness of open sky; over yonder a solid gloom of trees and, beyond, black houses with lighted windows; roofs, dingy roofs; below, blurred together, the garden; a chaos of tangled walls and all sorts of things; black houses with lighted windows and black windows; and, above me, the sky, vast, bluish, whitened with its early stars; mild air, no wind, air warm with the breath of early May. There is a warmth, a soft caress, in this velvety night air; the trees down there are a patch of gloom beneath the grey-blue circle of sky, spangled with tremulous gleams; and vague shadows brood in the garden of night. Ah, soft air, breath of spring, kind breath of summer nights! Leah, little Leah, my dearest, ownest, how I love her! Now all is merged in darkness; my dear one, lightly smiling, laughing lightly, how I love your eyes of laughter, those big eyes of yours, and tiny laughing mouth, your lips that smile! In shadows blurred the gardens stretch out beneath the clear sky, and I see your pretty golden head, your childish face, in teasing

54

mood, so delicately moulded, your golden hair and the pale bloom of your cheek, my laughing, smiling, teasing child . . . and how we love each other! To-night, on my dim balcony, against the dusk of distant walls, a vague elusive background of the night, in warm, dark air, I see your beauty and your grace; divinely graceful, as you move, the even cadence of your limbs; and languid your steps on the carpet beside the table with the flowers, in your delicious yellow room, yes, languidly you walk across a sheen of flowered softness, slowly leaning now this way, now that, palely smiling, your ivory face framed in frolic gold, smiling, slowly swaying as you pass, you pass before me; your light gown of creamy muslin floats about you, rippling where a ribbon flutters, gathered muslin moulding your bosom, your limbs, the young grace of your body; and softly your lips are moving; lovedear, I love you so. Tall shadows of trees climb skywards, high on high; and mine, all mine, you glimmer in the pale shadows, smiling, simple, sweet and kind; I love you purely . . . Her love is all I ask for, and then her embrace, but only as her love's free gift . . . I have had her body, yes, she yielded it,

55

but not her love! . . . Night, a darkness of trees,
sparkle of waxing stars; the rising night; the
room is behind me; I do not see her but I feel she
is there; behind me the heavier air of the room;
here freshness, mildness of the open; I must leave
this window now; ah, what an effort it is to tear
oneself away, to busy oneself about things, to do
things, and how good it would be to dream on
and on, in the farniente of the night, of my love
and my beloved, watching at this window the
tranquil dusk; to dream of a love for ever pure
and my beloved inviolate, a night of chastity;
good it would be still to dream in this calm ease
of evening! Before me, cool, dark night, night
cooler, darker yet; behind, the hot, relaxing
room, with its limpid candlelight; outside the
air is cool, within it is softer, warmer; outside is
coolness, almost cold; but soon so much darkness
saddens, it hurts to peer into that vast immo-
bility, the ghostly sky, that patch of gloom, the
trees; those gleams are cold as ice; almost funereal
this silence; I am afraid of the vast, soundless
night; indoors there is warm languor, relaxing
warmth of tapestry and carpets, safe walls and
yielding, comfortable things. Indoors! I pull

myself up and turn. The candles on the mantelpiece are lit; over there my white bed, downy
soft, the carpeted floor; I lean against the open
window and surmise the outer darkness of the
night behind me; black, cold, sad, funereal
night, shadows of fluent forms, a silence murmurous with rustling sands, tall trees massed in
darkness, bleak walls, dark windows of the
unknown and lighted windows, unknown too;
in the pale sky a flutter of tearful eyes, the stars;
thick black shadows that keep their secret,
merging in a shape of terror, yes, I feel it out
there, the unknown, the terrible. Shuddering,
I swing round hastily, seize the windows, tug
them, slam them to. Safe! . . . The window's
shut; the curtains now; I draw them together;
and night is blotted out. My room welcomes
me with its friendly glow; ah, it's good to be in
one's own room! This cosy room of mine, safe
from the perils of that empty darkness; comfort,
light. I lean against the wall. Now I am re-
assured, cheerful, secure; pale light of candles,
palely golden; soft feel of carpets and upholstery;
it's so inviting, cheery, comfortable. I shall
enjoy changing here, in this little room, this

snug little room of mine. My dressing-room is flooded with radiance, flashing white, the white of marble and running water. Well it's really time to dress now; let's see; I'm wearing my grey trousers and black coat; might go to Leah's in this rig, she's seen me in it often enough; it will do very well. A long coat? No, Leah will be alone. No need to change my boots; all the buttons on? Yes. Not dirty? Hardly, a flick of the brush will do. But I must change my shirt; that one, wore it yesterday, is quite clean; cuffs and collar haven't a trace; oh what a fag it is, changing! Still needs must, I suppose. Supposing, supposing, this night of nights, in Leah's room . . . well it might be to-night! Ah, the dear girl, if this night she were to . . . Devil take it, I must be going off my head! High time to start dressing; first of all, a clean shirt; my coat, there, on the bed; next, waistcoat, on the bed; now for the dressing-room; it's really very tidy, quite a good servant, that fellow; the candles are reflected in that wide glass above the dressing-table; straw-coloured walls; the big basin, white, filled with water; a few drops of musk in it, just a couple; shirt on the peg; it's a good thing I don't wear flannel shirts, they look ridiculous; the sponge; cold on the hand the water is; my head down in the water, brrr! Fine sensation that, one's head down in cool splashing water that gurgles slippery sliding all over it; one's ears buzzing, full of water, eyes closed first, then open in the greenness, skin tingling all over; sort of a thrill it gives one, almost like a caress. The sea this summer, delightful to look forward to; I suppose we will stay at Yport, mother likes that coast; those woods, the cliffs! Head plunged in the basin, sponge spurting water on my neck, cool ripple of the good water, just a hint of perfume in it, along my chest; towel now; got shaved about noon, that will have to do for the day; if only I was a dab at shaving; but, there, one never shaves oneself well and I'd look hopeless with a beard. Presentable now; yes, one should always be prepared; I shall be at Leah's to-night, and supposing, just supposing she asked me to stay the night, great that would be . . . I wonder, I wonder . . . Where's the hairbrush got to? It's curious how women of easy virtue can put up with any Tom, Dick or Harry; oh, after all, we're not so particular our-

59

selves. A fine clean-up that was; capital; quick now, get my clothes on; might catch a cold; a white shirt; look sharp; sleeve-links, studs; nice the feel of this clean linen; no nonsense, must get on with it; the bedroom now; my tie; those braces are hideous, wonder what possessed me to buy them; waistcoat; watch in the pocket; my coat; forgot to dust my boots; oh, let it go; no, just a flick of the clothes-brush, it's only a speck of dust; once, twice, that'll do; can put my coat on now; is my tie straight? Yes, all's well and I am ready; I can go now; handkerchief, card-case; quite all right; what's the time? Half past eight only; no use starting so soon; better sit down there, in the easy-chair; a whole hour to wait. How quiet it is here! There's nothing to beat it, old chap, a little siesta in a comfortable chair, after a quarter of an hour dressing and a good wash in cold water . . .

$\mathcal{A}$s I HAVE nothing more to do, why
not think out a bit, think out seriously, I mean,
how I am to behave to Leah to-night? Obviously
I shall stay with her till midnight or thereabouts
and then go home; the important thing is to make
her understand why I choose to act like that, and
devilish difficult it is to explain. I don't like this
room; better move to the sitting-room. I stand up;
the candles on my desk; I can pace up and down
the room in front of the fireplace and the two
windows; better draw the curtains first; and so
let's walk, taking it easy, up and down the room.
Now what is it I have to think about? Maddening the way when I want to think things out I
seem to get side-tracked at once. Ah yes, I've
got to fix up a programme for to-night; can't just
let things drift; I simply must make Leah under-

stand . . . The first thing is to find an oppor-
tunity for going away of my own accord;
several times when she hasn't asked me to stay it
really looked when I left as if I was being shown,
politely but firmly, the door! This evening, perhaps, she will consent to let me stay; suppose
she does; then I shall tell her of course it's best
that I should leave her; why should I stay if she
doesn't love me enough to keep me of her own
accord? That's what I'll say. But it's hard; doubt
if I can bring it off; she'll think it deuced queer
and stare at me with those big eyes of hers, full
of exaggerated surprise, half laughing at me,
like the day when I started to scold her; those
sudden little ways she has of darting to and fro
and her little gestures alert one moment, then
lazy like; that day when she flung her hat on the
flower-vase, her pearl-grey hat it was; how she
started laughing, laughing! Mad girl! There,
I'm off again; never seem able to stick to one
idea; really I'm a hopeless case. Supposing I
wrote it down; good notion; I'll make a book of
the words, what I am to say to her; anyhow it
will clear up my ideas a bit. I sit down. Blotter,
paper, ink, pen; nib seems all right; now for it.

In front of me the panel of Chinese silk, vague white flowers and among them, couchant, a stately stork with beak uplifted; smooth black silk; white-embroidered. Paper in the blotter; good; now I can start. What was it she said in her last letter? Better read it again; I've got her letters somewhere; yes, in the drawer, a whole bundle of them. Here's the entire collection, hers and rough drafts of mine. Her first letter, four months old now.

Dear Sir,
    It is quite impossible for me to accept your kind invitation for this evening, but I shall be free to-morrow if that will be convenient.
                Yours truly

That was the evening I asked her out to supper; I'd seen her the day before for the first time and at midnight I'd gone to the stage-door attendant to enquire if I could see her; he handed me this note. Next day? Next day it was she informed me that she hadn't any use for me; it was in this same janitor's den. Here's her next letter, a fort-night later.

Dear Mr Prince,

I am very much obliged for the service you so kindly . . .

I had called at her place; when one has set about something, one can't bring oneself to drop it all of a sudden; I tried all sorts of devices, tipping, writing; it would have been absurd to give it up, leave it at that, forget her. Louise was her maid then; how many louis I've had to give that fat damsel of hers! For those two weeks while Leah was away I had to content myself with interviewing that domestic treasure, Louise. Then came that queer business: Mademoiselle d'Arsay stranded somewhere or other in the Champagne district, without a sou; that morning I had got my six hundred francs from father; it must have been instinctive, that desire of mine to impress her, to shine in her eyes, make a splash; anyhow I gave her a cool three hundred; think, to a woman I had only seen twice, who'd slammed the door in my face; the handsome touch, you see, and, well, it certainly brought us together. Then she wrote that second letter.

I am very much obliged for the service you so kindly rendered me. If I had known sooner that it was to you I owed this generous act, I would have thanked you at once.

She had put *sooner*, struck it out and written at once.

But I have only just come to know of your generosity. So I am writing now to let you know I shall be back in Paris on Wednesday evening and if you will give me the pleasure of a visit on Thursday afternoon I shall be delighted to see you. Till Thursday then, and kindest regards from

yours

Leah d'Arsay

I had the notion then of entering in a note-book day by day the progress of my affair with Leah; I should have kept it up; it would have made interesting reading; even this three weeks' record is quite a curious document in its way; those were the three weeks, as it happened, which followed Leah's return to Paris, the early days of our liaison; my diary begins the day after she got back.

Thursday, January 27th. *Four o'clock; I go to the Rue Stévens; Leah receives me; white dress; tells me of her troubles, the rent unpaid; I offer to bring her two hundred francs at midnight; agreed.*

Midnight. *She comes back from the theatre with her mother and asks me into her room; a bit snappish at first; I hand her the two hundred; she won't let me stay, pretext — feeling out of sorts; manner more amiable, however.*

Obviously, having begun, I was bound to go on with it; it certainly looked as if this second donation would break down her resistance; I could hardly refuse it and lose all the ground gained by that first act of munificence.

Friday, January 28th. *Sent her white lilac.*

Saturday, January 29th. *Fancy I saw her in a carriage in the Rue des Martyrs; I go to Rue Stévens but Louise says she is dining out. I say that I will return at one o'clock next day.*

Sunday, January 30th. One o'clock. *Louise says she has gone to the country for some days; her mother insisted on it; she is absolutely under her mother's thumb, it seems; I make no secret of my exasperation*

66

and announce that I am leaving Paris for a week;
I've found out the allowance the consul used to make
her, five hundred francs a month; dresses and presents
as well.

January 31st to February 12th. Travelling in
Belgium.
February 5th. I write to her.
February 9th. Receive her reply.
February 10th. I write again.

I have the rough drafts of my two letters, and
her reply. This is my first letter.

I had hoped to see you before leaving on Monday
. . . And so on. A dull letter.

Her reply now.

I am greatly touched by the kind things you say
and I think you meant them sincerely. At your last
visit, you say, I seemed sad; I am feeling sad. I
suppose you could see I had something on my mind.
I did not dare to tell you, but just now I am going
through a very, very difficult time and I can't stop
brooding over it day or night. I have some very
pressing obligations to settle and, till I can get them
off my mind, I can neither be myself, nor yours. Unluckily I have no private means at all and I have such

heavy expenses to meet; though I cannot help feeling drawn towards you, I am too straightforward to hide from you any longer exactly how I stand. I know nothing of your circumstances and I've no idea of the sacrifices you could make at once to rescue me from the dreadful position I am in. After reading this please ask yourself if you can undertake to be my true friend in need; or else, if you prefer, forget all I have written and forget too

your

Leah d'Arsay

My second letter.

February 10th, 1887

My dear Leah,
I am very glad you have been so frank . . .

I wrote that I could help her but was somewhat alarmed by the extent to which she was involved. These first two letters were pretty formal; I watched my words.

My diary now.

Sunday, February 13th. *Went to Leah's place. Louise says she is ill in bed; wouldn't take her purgative, it seems; appointment for tomorrow.*

Monday, February 14th. *Half past one. Leah consents to see me; pale blue dress; I stay an hour, ask her about her worries; I offer to bring her ten louis in the evening; agreed, I am to come at eleven on condition that I leave at once, on account of her mother.*

11 P.M. *Shown into the dining-room. Her mother has invited some ladies without warning, it seems; impossible to let me stay; she assures me she's not to blame; I mustn't get angry; another time, she swears; she is nicer to me than ever before; I kiss her, a long kiss; leave after ten minutes; gave her the ten louis; another appointment for Wednesday.*

Wednesday, February 16th. *Rue Stévens, two o'clock; she was just going out; I stay half an hour in her room; she puts on her coat and hat; we fix up to dine somewhere to-morrow or the day after.*

Thursday, 17th. *One o'clock, Rue Stévens; I stay an hour and a half; we take coffee together; a street musician outside; we dance; her skirt comes loose and she leaves me to fix it up; the bell rings; she tells me it is the coalman with his bill; we come to an understanding; I settle the bill on condition that she receives me at one to-morrow. If I can't rely on you, she says, there's an end of it.*

69

Friday, 18th. *Nine o'clock. Louise alone; Leah is dining out; will return very late; a letter for me.*

Let's have a look at the letter.

February 18th.

Very sorry to be out this evening. You know how I am placed and that I can't do as I like; if I could have counted on what you promised I should have stayed. But I simply must find some way out of the difficulty I am in — and quickly. May I depend on you to help me, yes or no? If, as I believe, you have kept your word, please hand Louise what you would have given me and on Sunday at one o'clock I shall be here to thank you.

Curious girl! She lets me down because she thinks I'll not bring anything for her and then asks me to give something to her maid. Let's file these letters in their places.

Friday, 18th. *Nine o'clock . . . Leah is dining out . . . a letter for me.*

That was the letter.

I refuse to give money; entreaties from Louise; promises; Louise begs me anyhow to consider her; she has a baby girl with a wetnurse at Auteuil and can-

not pay the woman till she gets her wages; Leah is very worried, she says. I tell her point blank that Leah takes me for a fool and I'll not give her a sou till she has kept her word. On leaving I give Louise twenty francs.

And that's the end of my documentary evidence. A pity! For that's only the beginning of the story. Next Saturday what happened? Ah, that was the day she consented, at last, to give herself to me; a fine, sunny afternoon, I remember; I gave her the two hundred francs she wanted; pretty stiff price that for one embrace, but it's the devil of a business once one is properly entangled to break free; and, of course, it would be the same thing over again with another girl and all the leeway to make up as well; I had to stick to my guns, dogged does it, and yes I've nothing to regret. She took the precaution of locking the drawing-room door; I had just two hundred and five francs on me; I sent her roses that evening; that was the first time I bought them at Hanser-Harduin's; pretty shop-assistant they have there, she has a fascinating trick of seeming to laugh up her sleeve at one; I must go there again to buy flowers one of these days; really fetching, that little flower-girl.

Dear Boy,

You really must come . . .

An appointment, this,

I am so sorry I shall not be in to-morrow . . .

. . . a rehearsal to attend . . .

. . . come Monday at four . . .

. . . be together for a bit . . .

Another letter.

It's always the same bother, in my present straits I cannot do as I would like . . .

. . . simply dreadful . . .

. . . I absolutely must get straight somehow or other . . .

Then, damn it, that atrocious ultimatum of mine! That letter spoilt everything; how on earth did I ever write it? No doubt, the way I'd been behaving for the past month led up to it, worse luck — but why, oh why did I write it?

My dear girl,

I told you you could count on my help, but only to a limited extent. If I had large means I would beg you to accept whatever you needed to meet the expenses of your establishment. Forgive me if I say I am surprised when you speak of — more generous assistance. What I have done for you is nothing beside what I would wish to do, but do you think it is a mere bagatelle to me? And you, for the last two months, what have you done for me? You held out hopes of something better than the single hour you accorded me one afternoon. I am unable to come to-morrow before five; please send me a line to know if I may return after dinner. In that case you can count on my help. Au revoir, then, and believe me . . .

Tuesday Morning

Very grateful for your kind remarks. I am sorry you cannot come at one to-morrow; I will stay in for you till two. You know quite well that I am not free to do as I'd like; there is a certain person in my service I must get rid of, but to enable me to dismiss her I need a hundred and fifty francs to-morrow evening; once she is out of the way, I shall be much freer to do what I want. You see the position, I hope. So do try and bring the needful to-morrow and you will be able to judge for yourself how urgent it was for me to take this drastic step. To-morrow then

I hope to see you or get a line from you saying you will come to my assistance.

Ever yours . . .

Tuesday, two o'clock.

My dear,

I have just come home and read your letter. Were you offended at what I wrote yesterday? I felt absolutely desperate at the time. But surely you must admit that you have treated me very badly; it was you who drove me into being aggressive. I assure you all this makes me utterly miserable. I fancied you might learn to love me a little; when I realized that it was a hopeless dream I said to myself: So much the worse, then I'll go about it as the other fellows do . . . Do forgive me, and forget! I will come this evening; please be kind and do not send me away; I will bring you whatever you need. Let's have done with all these sordid worries and then you will see how deep my love is for you . . .

That evening at nine she was out; she had got my letter but left no message. I had lost her! Threats, anger and then a plea for forgiveness! And to think, oh to think that she might have learned to love me if I had tried to win her love in the right way!

74

Tuesday, March 1st, 11 P.M.

Ah yes, this is the set speech I composed; I'd been out for a long walk and here, alone, decided to prepare what I would say to her when we met next day.

Tuesday, March 1st, 11 P.M. *In her room, holding her in my arms, I shall say to her: — You do not believe in my love? . . . Oh if only what I am about to do might bring some solace to her poor, troubled heart! . . .*

That was written the evening after I had encountered in the street that girl with big, secret eyes, walking so wearily in her humble working-girl's dress under the bare trees; in the cool clear air of that March evening I passed close beside her, and she looked at me; a vague languor in her eyes; without a gesture, timidly, she glanced at me and passed . . . and then I thought of that other girl, my beloved, my beautiful, and all the sorrow of her poor, troubled heart! There was a wood fire burning here; outside the sky was cold, bright, clean-swept; no wind; a deep sky, far away; and in that bright air all things seemed mounting up towards the zenith; indoors,

kind warmth of the fireside, my solitude and memories.

— *You do not believe in my love?*

... *Oh if only what I am about to do might bring some solace to her poor, troubled heart!* ...

— *Dearest, I have thought deeply of all that has passed between us; I desired you — passionately; that is my only excuse; I forced myself on you and now I ask you to forgive me. I might pass this night in your arms, dear, but — . Good-bye, beloved, I give you back your body and I leave you now . . . because I love you.*

Then I will take her head in my hands, look into her eyes, and kiss her lips.

— *Good-bye* . . .

Those were the words to say; an end of cruel importunities. But I never had a chance of saying those words.

My dear boy, I absolutely must see you. Come this evening at ten. Yours, Leah.

What happened that night? Wasn't that the time she was ill? Ah yes; the night I spent at her bedside. Worn out she was, her nerves all on edge, collapsed, gasping for breath. I'd waited

some time for her to come home; she was in a
terrible state and went straight to bed; I
watched over her; we put compresses on her forehead; then she sent the maid away and alone I
looked after her; I spent the night in an easy
chair; she lay motionless and silent, utterly ex-
hausted, and I was lost in a dream of tenderness
and pity. She woke early, eight o'clock; I drew
back the curtains and she smiled to me. That was
the best moment of our love, the most wonderful
of all. She felt better in the afternoon; I spent a
quarter of an hour with her. And next day? It
was next day that she was so aggressively cheerful, laughing, singing, talking at the top of her
voice.

*Mademoiselle Leah d'Arsay will be delighted to
go to the Opera to-morrow with Monsieur Daniel
Prince. Kindest regards.*

How pretty she was that evening at the Opera
in her pink satin dress and white shoes! Chavainne was obliged to admit she looked pretty;
yes, even that contradictory fellow, Chavainne!
And that night at the Odéon; a tragedy they
played, *Andromaque.* Leah wanted to see some

new actress play, forget the name; funny idea of hers. We dined at Foyot's and she ordered widgeon; I was a fool not to give a big enough tip but luckily Leah didn't spot it; silly all the same; from that private room looking on to the Luxembourg we could see the students passing; she had her velvet dress, her jade-green hat with the red feather; and that serene, great-lady air she always assumes in public. Every night I used to see her home, say good-night and leave her; good days those were; once or twice she wanted to say good-night on her doorstep, but I always stuck out for ten minutes together in her flat. Now it's become a habit and those are really delicious moments we spend talking together in her room.

Louise's letter; a baroness's coronet on it.

Sir,

Monsieur Prince you once asked me to tell you if at any time Mademoiselle was in difficulties so I write to say she is very upset just now. A hundred and forty francs is due on the furniture. She never stops crying and they say that if the bill is not settled to-morrow evening all the things will be carted away and Mademoiselle Leah says if it comes to that she will feel quite desperate. I spoke of you but she says you cant do anything for her. I promised her to go and tell you of her worries but as I know I shall never be able to find you I thought it best to write without letting on to Mademoiselle Leah. If we are so lucky as to be helped by you I kindly beg you to say nothing to Mademoiselle Leah about it, because of what you told her last Sunday she forbade me to ever write to you. Please excuse me making bold to trouble you.

Yours truly

Louise

A card from Leah.

Mr. Prince's lovely flowers are much appreciated. Will he come to-morrow, Monday, at one p.m.?

Another letter.

Dear Daniel,

May I once again ask you to come to the rescue and be so kind as to let me have the trifling sum of forty or fifty francs, which I urgently need to-morrow? I'd be delighted if you could bring this yourself. Thanks, in anticipation, and my kindest regards.

Another card.

Leah d'Arsay asks to be excused by her friend Daniel Prince; his letter came too late for her to

*accept his kind invitation; but she will be delighted
to see him very soon and will write to fix the date.*

Another.

*Leah d'Arsay will have much pleasure in dining
with Monsieur Prince this evening and will be waiting for him at seven o'clock.*

Ah, here's something longer; the letter she
wrote a week ago about the jewellery.

Dear Boy,

*If I am to save my jewellery do please let me have
two hundred francs; it's pledged for that amount. If
only you will be so kind as to do this for your little
friend Leah she will be very, very grateful; it would
break her heart to see all her poor little trinkets go
under the hammer. If the money is not forthcoming
they will be sold up the day after to-morrow, Tuesday; I have just received the notice. Do please be nice
about this and I shall grow fonder and fonder of my
dear boy, my only true friend in the world. Marie will
call to-morrow to hear what you decide.*

A boring business that was; the jewels were
pledged for only a hundred and twenty francs
and there was in reality a fortnight to run. I paid
up the hundred and twenty; she hasn't asked me

81

for any money since then; that was a week ago; she's sure to be wanting some more soon; let's hope not too much; my finances are getting in a bad way with all this money spent on her.

Dear Boy,
I heard when I got back . . .

Her last letter, this; the day before yesterday.

. . . I heard when I got back that you had come to see me; unluckily I was out. You can make sure of seeing me if you come at one or half past one to-morrow, Sunday. I shall stay in so be sure to come. Ever yours,
Leah.

Of course I went to see her and she was kindness itself, all smiles, almost tender. And then . . . what on earth possessed me? Somehow, at one moment, I pressed her passionately in my arms, too passionately. She looked up at me and I murmured *Leah!* — I couldn't keep the passion out of my voice. Really I seem to have no self-control, always go too far. Leah seemed surprised; not angry, just surprised; a bit amused too, I think; but, damn it, why does she look so bewitching then? It's her fault; she's so pretty, so terribly fetching in those loose light dresses of hers; no, black really suits her best, that plain black close-fitting satin dress moulding her all-too-tranquil bosom . . . Good Lord, it's nearly half past nine; time to be moving. And I've not written down what I'm to say to her! Oh, never mind, it doesn't matter; I shall remember and, besides, I've got what I wrote a month ago. Up; my hat; gloves in overcoat; all in order here? Letters into the drawer. Wait, better read it over before I start out.

In her room . . . I shall say . . . You do not believe in my love? . . . I desired you — passionately; that is my only excuse . . . forgive me. I might pass this night in your arms, dear, but — . . . I give you back your body. Good-bye.

Good-bye, good-bye, time to go. Gas will be alight on the landing; I open the door, put out the candles; ware collisions now; all's well; door closed; down the stairs; my gloves; clean, yes, quite all right. Why, deuce take it, of course I shall remember, I've got it pat, what I'm to say to Leah; nothing easier, nothing simpler; and so she will understand why I don't take advantage of my rights over her, how truly I love her and why I do not ask to possess her body . . . I might pass this night in your arms, but — . . . I leave you now, dear . . . She will understand; nothing simpler, nothing easier . . . I desired you . . . passionately . . . *Très bien* . . . I give you back your body . . . because I love you.

The STREET, the black street with its double file of gaslamps, rising, diminishing; an empty street, resounding pavement, white under the whiteness of a cloudless sky and of the moon; far back, over there, the moon; a slim white fragment of the white moon; on both sides those everlasting houses, dumb, enormous, with tall, grimy windows, iron-bolted doors, houses; and in the houses, what? People? No, silence. Alone I walk beside the houses; silently, alone, I

walk, I pass. On the left the Rue de Naples and
garden walls, dark stains of leaves on the grey of
walls; down there in the distance a glow of
brightness, the Boulevard Malesherbes; red and
yellow lights, carriages, carriages with their
proud horses; along the streets, in calm repose,
carriages becalmed between the pavements and
hurrying crowds; a new house building here,
scaffolding daubed with plaster, dull-coloured;
can't make out the last stones they have laid,
layer on layer; I'd like to climb up those masts,
to that roof, what a height! and listen to the
noises of Paris far below; a man coming down
the street, a workman; there he goes; it's
lonely here, lonely and forlorn; a backwash,
no life, no traffic; the end of the street; here's
the Rue Monceau; more of those tall, stately
houses with the yellow light of the gaslamps
on them; someone in the doorway there, who?
The concierge of the house, smoking his pipe,
watching the passers-by; nobody to watch,
except me; what is he up to, that burly old
concierge, staring at nothing? In another street
now; narrow all of a sudden, seems to shrink
together; old houses, limewashed walls; chil-

dren on the pavement, street-urchins, squatting
on the ground, not saying a word; the Rue
du Rocher next and, beyond, the boulevards;
light there and noises; traffic there; the files of
gaslamps, right and left; at my side, on the left,
a carriage drawn up under the trees; a group of
workmen; a tramcar, that conductor has a tram-
full; the horn and he's off with a couple of dogs
after; lighted windows in the houses; opposite
me white curtains of a café, transparent; an
omnibus rumbling past; a girl, pink face, dark
blue dress; the crowd; the boulevard; presently
I shall be down there, amongst all those
people; I shall be there, the same I still, myself there, no longer here, I all the while; high
in front, the Butte; gleams under the clear sky;
on the right a long wall, the reservoir wall; I
know none of these people, do they see me, what
do they take me for? Shouts of children at play;
wheels lumbering down the causeway; sluggish
horses; a flight of steps; sky blotted out where the
trees are thicker; my footsteps on the asphalt,
monotonous, level; a quaint old song, probably
a dance tune, a sort of a waltz, in slow three
time . . . where's that hurdy-gurdy, now? I

can hear it droning away somewhere behind there, shrill yet soft . . . *For I love my turkeys and my geese, But oh I love you more* . . . a song, ending, beginning again, the same tune . . . cadence of a calm voice heard in some quiet countryside, call of a heart serene, a lover's; deep, secret longing of a voice that rises; and another voice in answer, higher and in unison, soaring serene and clear, up and up, winged with passionate desire; and now again the first voice soars with passion rising, and from their hearts, simple as the simple scene, upswells monotonous, alternate, that hymn of gentle melancholy; a soft, artless melody that grows, to an artless rhythm; among the cool leafage, against the burden of mingled sounds, a delicate voice, a melody, shrill yet soft, is sounding; a litany in monotone, to the steady rhythm of a slow dance; and love, love is born . . . In the virgin fields — but more than my fields, dear, *oh I love you more!* I watch the pale beauty of the fields and flocks that wander in them; but *oh I love you more!* Good they are to see, the flocks in my cool pastures, my flocks and herds of honest beasts; *I love you more!* Lovely they are to me, my dream-meadows, but

I love you more, and your bright eyes; lines of lights and tree-trunks stretch out before me; but *oh I love you more* when you are singing; a river of shadows flowing past under the night-sky, far-away noises, remoter yet the singing voice; artless voice and rhythm grow fainter and fainter; their evensong is over; but more than any song, than all the melodies of love, I love you; cool night around me, and the long lines of trees, footsteps of passers-by, rumble of traffic; spoken words, hues enshadowed; a gentle, warmer air; I will go to the wood which skirts the hill beside the meadows, under the fir-trees, and yield myself to the warm languor of those delicious nights. We will all be there, lovely climate it is, far away from Paris, for weeks and weeks. But, when, I wonder? . . . Noisier here, Place Clichy; must hurry up; always those gloomy lines of walls; thicker shadows on the pavement; ah, here we have the afterdusks, three of them, chatting together; they haven't noticed me; she's quite young that one, slender, bold eyes; killing, the lips she has! In a bare room, shapeless, high up, grey and bare, by smoky candlelight, where all the noises of the street are muted; yes, a high, narrow room, low bed, chair, table, grey walls; and in the ruck of the bed a kneeling beast, with roving, lustful lips, a panting, groaning creature . . . Near her now; she's talking; the three of them on the pavement together, not attending to customers; to-morrow, deuce take it, there's that lecture to attend, my course; in three months the exam: — of course I shall get my pass; good-bye to freedom then; have to buckle down to my job; hullo, regular covey of the girls I've run into here; the café; young people going in; that fellow is like my tailor; supposing I met some pal; but it's better to be alone to roam the streets on a topping evening like to-night, just as one pleases, anywhere. Shadows of leaves restless now on the asphalt, a cool breeze has sprung up; the pavements are shining, bone-dry; over there a party of young girls, tall, slender; fascinating they look there; some children, too; the house fronts are sparkling, the moon has set; a murmur in the air; it's vague sounds all mixed up, a murmur . . . A lovely month, April! And what a joy to-night to drift along like this, just as one pleases, thinking of nothing, alone, all alone!

Rᴜᴇ Sᴛᴇ́ᴠᴇɴs, and Leah's house at
last; here is the hall; staircase now, the winding
stairs; and this should be the second floor;
yes, here we are. My boots are clean, tie's
straight, moustache turned up; good. What a lot
of things I'm going to tell her, so many things I've
got to say! Let's see, she must have just got
back; she'll be wearing that black cashmere
dress; here, I'm a fool not to ring at once; sup⁓
posing she spotted me dawdling here; I ring;
footsteps behind the door; it's opened; Marie.

— Is Mademoiselle d'Arsay at home?

— Yes, sir, please come in.

I enter.

— I will tell Mademoiselle that you have
come.

Nice girl, Marie. This room is really charming,

mony of lissom curves, the grace supreme of softly yielding flesh, a dim, elusive loveliness; her young face is reposeful now and a sigh rises from her parted lips . . . The candles flicker on the mantelpiece, their flames rise, palely yellow, faint blue, then brighter; but round us is a shadowed twilight of dark foliage, a dim disorder of painted china, and, behind, in the vague lustre of the mirror, reflections reconciled . . . That was a capital ball I went to in the winter; the room was full of flowers and foliage, tactful lighting; and there were those two English girls who passed beside me, those snow-white girls . . . A warm profusion of things is here, and my beloved near me; a warmth, little by little, is growing in her motionless body; a fervour permeates her body and mine caressed by hers. If she is so unhappy, why does she refuse to start a new life? . . . How grateful, comforting this warmth of her body and her perfume! A mixture of scents, subtly keen, blended together, all she is with all she has, by her blended; the perfume flows from all her body, from her clothes, a waft from the braided tresses of her hair, from her lips as well. She is asleep, my lovedear, in

my arms, and I am ravished by her fragrance, that
blended, subtle, intimate scent with which she
impregnates her body, infused with her body's
own perfume; I can distinguish it, her own, her
body's own perfume, from all those mingled
essences of flowers; yes, a tang of womanhood,
the woman's mystic emanation at her hour of love,
when sensually, with what ecstasy, at her man's
bidding, the dark passion of her flesh is effused in
an embrace, in love's orgastic madness, a pale
swoon of terrible delight! What joy, that to
enjoy, ah joy indeed . . . ! She moves her head,
half turns away; have I pressed her too closely?
In a dream she whispers.
    — What's come over you? Oh, I'm so tired!
What time is it?
    — Early yet . . . Don't move . . .
    Now she is quiet again, so daintily alluring in
her young coquetry; a miserable life she has to
lead; and how strong his love needs to be, her
lover's love, to smooth the rough ways she has to
tread; only twenty, poor little girl, and already
she has learnt how cruel life can be! Ah, it's good
to be together like this and dream together, forgetting all, just we two; lulled, she by her trust

in me, I by her charm; together in a world of our very own, utterly happy . . . Soon we will go out under the shadow of the trees, in our ears a distant music . . . *For I love you* . . . *and you love me;* yes, not only *I love you,* but at last . . . *you love me* . . . a kiss now . . . *and you love me.* She is asleep. I'm nearly asleep myself, my eyes half-closed . . . this is her body; the rise and fall of her breast, her blended fragrance, oh lovely April night! . . . Presently we shall be driving together . . . in cool air . . . we will go out . . . quite soon . . . the two candles . . . there . . . along the boulevards . . . *I love my turkeys and my sheep, But oh I love you more* . . . That street-girl with the bold eyes and cherry lips . . . the room, high fireplace . . . the dining-room . . . my father . . . sitting together, we three, father, mother, I . . . why is mother so pale? . . . she is watching me . . . we shall dine, yes, in the garden . . . the servant . . . bring the table . . . Leah . . . she is laying the table . . . my father . . . the concierge . . . with a letter . . . a letter from her? . . . thanks . . . a ripple, a murmur, skies uprising, high on high . . . you, you alone of all beloved, from the

beginning, Antonia . . . glitter of lights every-
where . . . are you laughing? . . . lines of street-
lamps stretching out to infinity . . . night . . .
cold, icy night . . . Oh horror, this horror of
darkness! . . . What? . . . I'm being trampled
on, tormented, they are killing me . . . No
. . . a laugh again . . . the room . . . Leah . . .
Good Lord, was I dreaming?

— Congratulations, my dear . . . Leah is
speaking . . . Hope you enjoyed your nap . . .
Yes, it's Leah; she's standing there, laughing
. . . Feeling better now?

— Thanks, yes, and how do *you* feel?

Laughing she turns; now I laugh too; she is
walking up and down the room. She must have
waked a moment ago; saw I'd dozed off and
slipped away. I've gone and made a fool of myself, what's to be done? What ever must she
think of me! I get up and sit on the piano stool;
she is looking at herself in the glass over there;
gaily she asks:

— Didn't you go to bed last night?

— I believe I did, Mademoiselle, and had
quite a decent night's rest. It must have been that
hypnotic charm of yours . . .

— Well, shall we go out? It's such a lovely night. We might have an hour's drive along the Champs-Elysées. What do you say?

— An excellent idea.

— Only I hope you won't fall asleep on the way.

— No. You shall tell me stories.

— Thanks very much; I'm to provide the entertainment. You'd better write it all out, what I'm to do.

— Don't be unkind.

And some days, the Lord knows, I have my work cut out to get her to say a word.

— I'll just put my hat on.

She comes nearer and as she smiles I see the white flash of her teeth, the moist sparkle of her eyes, her rosy lips half parted, and in their tiny rose triangle inset a flash of whiteness. That forlorn air suits you to perfection, Mademoiselle, with those blush-rose-and-white dimples on your cheek, your forehead drooping above me in a poise of tender melancholy, your big eyes watching me.

— My poor darling, if only I knew how to make you happy!

104

I draw her towards me; her head is nestling on my shoulder; now my arms are round her waist and, unseen, I kiss her hair. Happy moment, for now she is kind, all loveliness, tenderness; kind and gentle is she . . . my darling, and to love her is an enchantment! She raises her head and observes me curiously, fixedly; she lifts her hand, invoking silence, why? She seems to be listening; then tenderly she asks me:

— What is the matter with you?

— Why do you ask?

— Are you feeling ill?

— Not a bit.

— Sure your heart isn't out of order?

Placing her hand on my left breast, she listens; and, now that I notice it, there is something queer about the way my heart is beating.

— Quite sure?

— There's nothing wrong, nothing, I assure you. You are there and so naturally I . . .

Gently she interposes . . .

— What a child you are!

So gently she whispers: *What a child you are!* . . . a quiet whisper of deep sincerity; and her smiling eyes grow earnest as she says *a child;*

105

from the depth of her heart, from her woman's heart, she is speaking: I am a child; and she moves away, adorable in her beauty.

— A couple of minutes, my dear.

She is at the door; yes, I say; she is gone.

— I'll put my hat on and come back.

The door is ajar; I sit down and wait; waiting, awaiting her.

— I'll tell Marie to call a carriage . . . Marie!

— Shall I go instead?

— No, Marie will go.

She is talking to Marie in the bedroom; what's that she's saying? Can't make out. I am doing nothing here; nothing to do. To-morrow I lunch with de Rivare at eleven; at one of the cafés on the boulevards, I suppose; pretty hard it is to keep an appointment at eleven or ten-thirty when one has been making a late night of it; the best way really to make sure of being up in time is to sleep out; here, for instance; why not? When all's said and done, what have I come here for?

— Ready.

Leah standing at the door; she is wearing her red velvet hat; her great lady's air — to amuse

me; I bow ceremoniously and she curtsies in reply; cab-wheels rumbling outside.
    — The carriage waits, she says . . . Let's go.
    — Sure you've forgotten nothing, Leah?
    — No; here's my cloak.
    — Let me take it . . . Thanks.
Over my arm her fur coat, warm, downy.
    — Your gloves? You've only one.
    — Ah yes, I was forgetting the other; it's on
the piano; you might fetch it.
    I knew she would forget something; told her
so.
    — Here it is.
Marie comes back.
    — The carriage is at the door, Mademoiselle.
    — I'll be back in an hour; please light the fire
in my room.
    — Good-night, Marie.
It would never do to forget to say good-night
to Marie. Leah is going down the stairs, the black
satin of her dress billowing round her; she is
walking down the stairs and I follow. At each
step her shoulders swing back and the red feather
in her hat sways downwards, upwards, down

again; she holds herself erect as she descends, slowly buttoning a long black glove on her left hand; in even rhythm she descends step after step, holding herself erect; here's the street; a faint ruddy glow; the carriage silhouetted black against the light.

— Aren't you risking a chill in the open carriage?

— No, it's quite fine tonight.

— Will you get in . . . ?

She gets in; I follow.

— Take care not to sit on my dress.

The unforgivable sin!

— Shall we go towards the Arc de Triomphe?

— Yes.

— Driver, follow the boulevards to the Arc de Triomphe.

I sit down; the carriage moves forward. Leah is looking so serious, so dignified, you'd think I was out driving with a leading lady from the Comédie Française.

𝒯HE CARRIAGE moving along the streets . . . A single one in the unnumbered host of lives, thus I go my way, one by distinction among the rest; and so the Now, the Here, this hour striking, this world of life, all these come to being within me . . . And what am I? A soul in flight towards a dreamland of kisses; the Now my dream of a fair woman, my Here her body touching mine, my hour this hour that brings us closer; and the dream of dreams, on which my heart is set, this girl to-night . . . Murmurous streets, the boulevard, muffled sounds, the cab moving with a rumble of wheels on the causeway, thudding, lurching onward, through the clear evening air, past streaming shapes on either hand, the two of us side by side . . . a heavenly night!

Leah is speaking.

— Isn't it simply entrancing to-night, a perfect poem?

As she was leaving Leah told her maid, yes that was it, that she'd be back in an hour and to have the fire lit. When we return I shall go up to the flat with her; more leaves out on the trees along this boulevard; I shall go upstairs with her, but I'll only stay a quarter of an hour and then I shall leave her, as I've decided I must do; now doesn't she look pretty leaning back like that, her face now lit up, now darkened; caught in a web of shadows, then under the white lamplight, as the carriage moves along; under the street lamps, of course, a pool of light and after we've passed them sudden obscurity; there, again; the gasjets on the right are brighter. Lovely her face is now, so white, ivory-white, dim-white, like snow in twilight, shrouded in darkness, and again whiter, brighter than the lights themselves; in shadows overcast, to brightness returning. Our cab is rolling over smooth woodblocks now; gently, within a fold of her dress, I clasp her fingers; she draws them a little away; I speak:

— Do you know, this play of light and shadow on your face is simply fascinating.

— Really? You don't mean it!

Her voice sounds mocking, bored rather, malicious. Oh, why has she these moods? Gently I insist.

— I mean it, Leah. Do you mind my telling you?

— Not at all. I love compliments.

Compliments! I can't let that pass.

— From me, Leah . . . compliments!

We are silent now; people are passing; the coachman brandishes his whip and the long lash flies out in zigzags; I have released Leah's hand; she often sulks when we go out together; wants to keep up appearances, I suppose; fond of shutting me up unless I address her in my best drawing-room manner; hullo, here's the reservoir wall; a little time ago I was walking past it, alone; now I am with Leah; she's getting peevish, but nothing I can say will do the least good. Tram coming; a black monster with eyes of fire. Leah is speaking.

— Are you going next Saturday to the Press bazaar?

— At the Hotel Continental?

— Yes.

— I haven't decided. Possibly. Will you be there?

— I've been asked to be one of the sellers.

— Really?

— Yes. Lucie Harel is running a sort of shop there, rather like the fancy goods department in one of the big stores, you know, selling all sorts of things.

— I'd heard something about it. It ought to be a good show. So you'll have a stall?

— Yes.

— Then I'll go.

The business will run me in for a hundred francs, I know. Wonder if I can find a pretext for dodging it; no; Leah'd never forgive me. Still I might hit on a good excuse — couldn't say I was ill, but I might invent an urgent engagement. Boring shows they are, those bazaars. Wait, I might bring Chavainne with me . . .

— Will you be in fancy dress?

— Yes, as a soubrette.

— Capital!

— I shall touch up the dress I wear in the Revue; but those flounces in the blouse are no good, I shall have to put something else there . . .

Yes, I remember that soubrette dress; pink satin, lace apron, short skirt.

— I'll wear a satin sash to match and have some ribbons on the sleeves; that'll make the dress look like new; but I must change the apron. I've an idea for a really fetching one.

— A new apron?

— I've used up the lace from the old one; it didn't suit. Don't you think that would be a good idea . . . just plain Valenciennes lace?

— Yes, certainly.

She is smiling at her thoughts; now I wonder, I wonder if she's going to ask me to . . .

— Valenciennes isn't really so dear, you know; it costs about fifteen francs a yard and three yards of lace insertion will be heaps.

The cat's out of the bag. Well, I'll buy her the lace and cut out the bazaar.

— That's a good idea of yours, Leah, and if you'll let me assist by supplying this bit of lace I'll be delighted.

— Many thanks. It's very nice of you.

Another four or five louis gone; her fifteen francs a yard will turn out to be nearer twenty or thirty; but I'm damned if I'll set foot inside that fancy fair of hers; better change the subject and put a good face on it.

— Your costume in the revue looked awfully well; it will be a great success again, you'll see.

— Do you think so?

— A lot of smart people go to these charity shows, you know.

— Yes.

— Have you any idea if there will be a big crowd?

— No idea.

— Really?

— How can I tell?

— I thought you might have heard . . . Will that be the only stall there — Lucie Harel's?

— It's going to be a huge affair, you know, like a shop.

— That was an amusing idea fitting it up to look like a real fancy shop; it will make a vast hit, you'll see.

She looks bored again; I can hardly get a word out of her. What shall I say now?

— Nothing of the kind has been done before, I imagine.

Silence. She has half-closed her eyes.

— You will look delightful in that dress —
still you'd better not ask too fancy prices for your
fancy goods! I wonder what sort of things you
will be selling. But mind you don't start flirting
with your customers or I shall be jealous.

The ghost of a mocking smile on her face.
My little witticisms are dull as ditchwater, I admit. Wish to goodness this drive were over!

— It's getting cold, Leah observes.

Pretending not to have heard what I said.

— You're feeling cold, Leah. Let's turn back.

— No, not yet.

Black trees, iron gates, gleams of blue; we are
passing the Parc Monceau; behind those gates,
under the trees, the promenades; a stroll in there
wouldn't be bad; I wonder if by any chance Leah
would . . .

— I say, Leah, how about stopping here and
walking about a bit? If you're feeling cold . . .

— No, I'm not cold; let's stay where we are.

No luck; no way of making her talk or do anything; the air's getting nippy, she'll be catching
a chill.

— Leah, do please put on your coat.

She rises, extends an arm; I help her on with

her fur coat; from her air of bored resignation you'd think I was doing violence to her! Now isn't she really much better like that; and fetching she looks in her furs! A swathe of fur round her neck; furry sleeves setting off her black-gloved hands; if only she would be nice, how nice she'd be! She is so delightful there, motionless, half buried in those rich materials, her face pale gleaming above all that velvet, silk and fur; if the Desrieux could see her now! Rather amusing it would be if someone I know happened to pass; those Desrieux would think no end of me if they saw me out with her; a very up-to-date lot they are but why ever do they persist in wearing those square-toed shoes? And de Rivare, if he met us now, why he'd be fairly bowled over! He'd chaff me about it to-morrow at lunch over a bottle of excellent wine; but he'd be terribly jealous of my luck, that's sure. Must ask him out to dinner one evening; we can go to the Cirque, no, the Nouveautés, then I shall have a chance of telling him about Leah. By the way, I really must say something to her; when she is silent, I never can think of anything to say; things that interest her one day bore her the next; I don't believe there's

117

another woman in the world so capricious as she; now what on earth shall I talk about? Her show? Deadly dull subject, but better than nothing.

— Will the rehearsals for your next show be starting soon?

— I don't think so.

— Why not?

— We've standing room only every night.

— Do you know what it's going to be called?

— Haven't an idea.

— I think you said you would come on only in the third act.

— I prefer appearing in only one act.

— Really?

— I can't understand the passion some people have for coming on in all the acts when one's not playing a lead. Last year that Manuela girl made a hit with her song in the third act. Then you have Darvilly who is much cleverer and prettier than Manuela — she really isn't up to much, Manuela, you know, just look at the way she acts in the present show, still, of course, it's a rotten play, I admit — well Darvilly is on half the time and no one takes any notice of her.

— That's partly her fault; she's not much good on the stage.

— She has a very agreeable voice and acts very well — much better than all your silly little walkers-on, really they're a hopeless crowd, those girls; you're always talking about actresses and singing and art, but when you come across someone who really knows how to act she might be in the moon for all the notice you take of her.

Better slip in a compliment here.

— But, my dear, the applause you get every evening seems to prove just the contrary.

She says nothing; not offended; that sort of compliment comes never amiss; touches the spot every time.

— Just look at that woman on the other side of the boulevard in a light dress. What an idea to be wearing light colours in this season!

Leah is pointing; on the other side of the boulevard, a smartly dressed woman in a light-coloured dress.

— Yes, it is a bit odd; but the effect's rather becoming.

— Perhaps, but, fancy, in this season . . . !

She looks at me, half smiling; quite taken aback she seems.

— I admit, it's out of the ordinary run.

— That's what I mean.

Foolish little Leah; she doesn't realize that I'm laughing at her and how absurd she is; growing indignant or excited about the veriest trifles; this afternoon she simply couldn't get over that story about Jacques.

— The streets are very empty to-night, she says.

— All the same it's a lovely evening.

— A bit chilly, though.

— I'm certain you are feeling cold. We'd better turn back.

— No. I'm not feeling cold at all.

Her obstinacy; she is cold but won't admit it; curious creatures women are! Yes, the air's decidedly chillier; in the trees there the wind is freshening; here is the Place des Ternes; we shall never get as far as the Champs-Elysées. Not a soul in sight on the boulevard; terribly gloomy the streets to-night; if we go to the Champs-Elysées we shan't be back before midnight or one o'clock.

— It's cold, Leah says. Shall we return now? At last!

— Driver, we'll go back; number 14, Rue Stévens.

The cabby pulls up; reined in, the horse moves stiffly as the carriage turns; homeward bound; trotting again; in even measure the cab vibrates to the horse's trot; again that monotone of movement; a long-drawn crack of the whip; another carriage catches us up, goes ahead; why are we moving so slowly? Two very old people on the pavement there; noise of the wheels; a gentle jolting; again the Parc Monceau, the rotunda; in a quarter of an hour we shall be back. What will Leah say to me? I shall accompany her in, yes I certainly must go in; with her I shall enter the bedroom; ah but will she let me? The other day she insisted on my leaving her at once; yes, but more often I stay till she begins to undress; must be careful to ask her leave to enter when we are at the door; she will get down first; she's on my right, the near side; yes, at the least she'll let me see her to her room. And then . . . what will she say, will she at last allow me to stay the

121

night? Most unlikely; and, in any case, I'd refuse
to do so; a quarter of an hour in her bedroom,
while she's taking off her coat and hat; that will
be splendid; but supposing she really wants me
to stay, after all she must guess that one day or
other she will have to let me, it's inevitable; it
looked as if she fixed things up so as to be free to-
night; ah, to-night if it were to be . . . ! Or not
to be. Anyhow she must make up her mind; she
can't imagine that this Platonic love business
will continue indefinitely; I've never led her to
believe that, far from it; and she mustn't imagine
she has such a hold over me that I will put up
with anything and everything for nothing in return; what a problem it all is! That long line of
lights is getting nearer, the Boulevard Malesherbes; always moving on, the carriage; but
why should she be more willing to-night than
yesterday? Over and over again she has managed,
tactfully of course, to show me the door; of course
I never asked anything of her, in fact I never
seemed to want anything; could hardly expect her
to propose that herself. That would be a great
occasion, simply wonderful, if some day she consented. She is here beside me, motionless. My

God, how utterly remote it seems, that hope of mine! She is beside me, motionless, indifferent, detached; vaguely she looks straight before her; her hands hidden in her coat; her eyes, unseeing, are fixed on the road ahead; through the silence of the night we are moving without effort; from the tall houses, half in darkness, falls the ruddy glow of windows; left of us the trees; on the roadway an even cadence of horsehoofs, the rhythmic trot of our dapple grey; and she beside me, motionless, lost in a waking dream, detached, remote, without movement, without love. Oh will it ever come, that day she freely gives herself to me, if still she is untouched by love, this pale girl at my side? But somewhere surely, in the depth of her heart, is kindling even now a spark, a furtive, humble spark of simple liking for me; surely all my devotion hasn't utterly failed; slowly love permeates the heart of the beloved and, like a magnet, desire attracts desire; perhaps already some regard for me is taking root in the depths of her being, ready to grow, to blossom into love; and, if to-night her voice is silent as her eyes, surely it's because that tenderness is taking form far away from lips and eyes, deep down in her heart! Then let me yield myself to my fond imagining, that some day I shall be loved by her, this child-woman at my side, whose body touches mine, a frail, uncaring child whose spirit is wandering now in a dreamland of no thoughts, under this starry sky, in the cool darkness. Along dim ways, by the hidden ways of far horizons, lulled by the cadences of our wandering dreams, to a soft undertone of turning wheels, the murmurous motion of this carriage, our fairy coach, we are moving homewards, and tenderly I turn and speak to Leah; and if I speak it is only that in the dusk a sound of words may rise.

— What are you dreaming of, dear?

She turns and looks at me; a pale look, void of thought; no answer; the carriage is thudding roughly now upon the road; again Leah looks straight before her, silent still; she is not dreaming, no, not musing; what are you dreaming of? Nothing. What are you dreaming of? Don't know. What are you dreaming of? I can't say. But tell me, tell me of what are you —— ? Nothing, I can't say, I don't know, I don't dream, I don't think . . . No, alas; and I, I cannot teach you that — to dream; thus for ever you will remain, unmoving, unloving. Vaguely she looks before her; in the clear sky, less clear now, a brightness lingers; and we are drifting between dark cliffs of trees; the grey form of the old cabby, bent-backed, thrones above us; and I hear Leah speaking.

— I hope to goodness Marie hasn't forgotten to light the fire.

— Feeling cold, dear?

— A little.

— Come close to me then.

Lightly she leans against me, bending her head, smiling.

— Good. Now you'll get warm.

— On one side, yes.

— Come closer then.

— Naughty boy, now behave yourself!

A gentle reminder; we are out of doors; must keep up appearances; yes, there are people looking; who is that smartly dressed man coming towards us, looking our way? Why is he staring at us like that? Can't take his eyes off us, confound him! Passing close beside the carriage now. Let's see if he turns back; no, he hasn't turned; what was he after? Wonder if Leah saw him; anyhow she gave no sign of it; that fellow certainly knows her; expect he's pretty sick, jealous of me; well, why not? It isn't everybody who can take Leah d'Arsay out for a midnight drive. Is he still in sight? Yes, down there; ah, now he's looking back; well, old chap, you can stare your eyes out under that elm-tree, and welcome!

— We're at the Place Blanche, Leah; nearly home.

The whip cracks in the air; the carriage rumbles on.

— See over there, Leah; looks as if that house was being pulled down.

— What is it, that house? A café?

Near home . . . nearly home, I said; near Leah's home; the critical moment is near, too . . . but I'm silly to get nervy like this, for no reason, all of a sudden; I have the prettiest little woman in the world beside me; we have been for a drive together and I am going to her place; what more can a fellow ask for? That man we passed just now must be sick to tears; yes, I'm the luckiest of mortals . . . No, I can't bear it, I can't bear it!

Stop that; I must be going off my head; of course, of course I shall bring it off, I'm simply bound to . . . Place Pigalle already; a regular Jehu this cabman; the Passage Stévens; in a minute we shall be at her door; Lord, oh Lord, if only I knew what she is going to say to me now! What is she going to do? What shall I do? Cab slowing down, turning; she will tell me to go . . . again! Her house, her room . . . The cab pulls up. Leah moves, alights. This unbearable suspense, it's killing me . . . oh my dear, my dear, to-night, at last, will you . . . ? Eh, what's this she's saying, standing there?

— Aren't you going to pay the cabby?

Forgotten; yes; very sorry; two francs fifty; here you are. Leah at the door, ringing; it's all up now; dear, I implore you . . .

— May I come in with you?

— If you like.

Thank heaven! Thank heaven! What a relief! . . . The cab's off; now I'll go upstairs with her; what time is it? Not midnight yet; plenty of time; when I get home late that concierge of mine always keeps me waiting hours on the doorstep to let me in, and a damned nuisance it is.

127

SHE IS LEADING the way upstairs; shadows along the pale walls, our shadows; how much money have I on me? In my card-case fifty francs, four louis in my pocket; fifty and eighty, that makes a hundred and thirty francs in all; more at home; all the same it will be a pinch at the end of the month; Leah mustn't overdo it; well, well let's make our way upstairs; here we are; door opened; Marie.

— Evening, Marie.

— Good evening, sir.

Leah speaks.

— You remembered about the fire, Marie?

— Yes, Mademoiselle; if Mademoiselle wishes to go to her room . . .

At the end of the hall the dressing-room door; her bedroom beyond; nonchalantly Leah moves

towards it, it's charming that casual way she has
of moving; shall I follow her or wait till she invites me in? No, it won't strike her to ask me
. . . but supposing she sends me away? Oh here
goes, a fool I'd look mooning in the hall; I
enter; let her scold me if she wants; I cross the
dressing-room; the bedroom door; a glow from
the wood fire beyond, light too from that hanging
nightlamp and the two candles on the little
table; Leah is seated in front of the fire; a white
alabaster radiance from the hanging lamp, and
over the blazing logs a bright, restless flicker of
dancing flame; she is in the easy chair, toasting
herself; hat, gloves still on; motionless she sits in
a patch of shadow; the upward flame of the twin
candles gleaming; on her dress a dull glint of
golden firelight; soothing, delicious it is in here.

— You felt cold, Leah, didn't you?

But I couldn't get her to come back sooner,
the obstinate girl!

— Hadn't you better take your hat and cloak
off?

She remains seated before the fire, in shadow
dappled with firelight; obstinate as ever she will
persist now, I suppose, in keeping her things on.

129

No, suddenly she stands up and speaks all in a rush.

— Yes, it's much too hot in here.

She takes her hat off and throws it on the bed; settles her hair, then removes her gloves and flings them too on the bed; I am leaning against the mantelpiece; she begins to unbutton her coat; I move to aid her.

— Thanks, Marie will help me.

Marie assists while I return to my place by the fire; Marie carries the coat away; this fire is scorching my calves. Smiling, Leah turns to me.

— How about you? Are you going to stay like that with your overcoat buttoned up and your hat in your hand?

What does she mean, I wonder? Wants me to take my coat off. Then why? To stay? Can it possibly be that . . . ? I murmur as, smiling still, she observes me.

— If you'll allow me . . .

Slowly she turns, slowly, with that lithe movement of her, towards the wardrobe mirror, opposite the fireplace; I place my hat, overcoat, on a chair near the window; hat above the overcoat; standing before the glass, Leah settles the

flounces of her blouse, the black ribbon round her
neck; I lean against the wall, beside the cur-
tained window, and in the glass I can watch her
pretty gestures, childish profile, all her body,
now hidden, now revealed by her dress; how
deliciously these modern creations conspire to
reveal and hide alternately a woman's figure!
There is a feline grace in her movement as she
comes towards me, ringlets flickering gold over
the soft whiteness of her brow. Yes, I wonder,
this evening will she . . . ? She told me to take
off my overcoat. And then . . . ? I move a step
nearer; now we are face to face, in her eyes I see,
I see a light of . . . love surely it is! Then I've
won? Has my hour come at last? Tenderly she
whispers.

— If you were very nice, you'd go to the
drawing-room now for just five minutes.

— Certainly, dear, if you wish it.

She takes a candlestick from the mantelpiece
and lights the candles. So it's true then, she has
yielded; I'm to await her here.

— If you'll wait just five minutes. Mind not
to play the piano.

She is closing the door.

— *Au revoir.*

So here I am back in the drawing-room again;
only an hour ago and how different it all was!
It's a certainty Leah will invite me to stay, sure
thing; otherwise why ask me to wait while she is
undressing? She's in such a kind mood this evening. There's no possible doubt about it, I'm to
stay the night. Why to-night, I wonder, rather
than another? Still . . . why not tonight? No
shadow of doubt, she wants me to stay; thrilling
this moment is! Fancy, in a few minutes she will
call me, I shall return to her room, hold her in my
arms, loosen those long scented silken garments
of hers, and presently . . . in her bed . . . !
Steady now, mustn't let my imagination run
amok, this business has got to be tackled with
prudence; better take my precautions while I am
alone; must be nearly six hours since that lavatory
in the Boulevard Sébastopol; the privy here is on
the left of the hall; one should feel at ease on these
amorous occasions; mind not to make a noise
though, mustn't be heard going out; the hall lamp
should be lit, anyhow I have matches; open the
door now; hush, no noise; tip-toe out; good business, the light's on; door's ajar; remember gen-

tlemen are requested to adjust; for this relief
—— and very needful it was; I leave the door
ajar as I found it; the drawing-room door; softly
does it; here we are; capital, no one can have
heard me; and now let's take it easy for a while
in this armchair. Leah is undressing; she'll change
into her dressing-gown; funny how she will never
even put a shoe on or take it off when I'm looking.
What time? Quarter to midnight; Leah is pretty
quick at changing, she'll call me in a minute.
That's silly now; only two hours ago I was re-
hearsing what to do, why it's a month since I
fixed it up, and now it's gone clean out of my
head; simple enough, all the same; Leah wants
me to spend the night with her; very well, I
must refuse, and prove my love for her in the
best way, by honouring that love and refusing
the gift of her body, the gift she feels obliged
to offer me; by declining to imitate those others,
slaves of their blind passion; by loving her
with all my heart and asking of her only love;
that is it; I will not accept the sacrifice she is
ready to make, but myself will sacrifice myself . . . But supposing she felt offended? No,
I'll explain why I am leaving her and she will

be touched. Damn it! What a coward, what a fool I am! The long-awaited moment has come and here I am wobbling between two minds; no, I'm not, not really; why, it's simplicity itself; I have to choose whether to possess this girl in a vulgar night of passion or keep my love intact, winning hers into the bargain, perhaps; no need for windy rhetoric, dramatic gestures and the rest of it; presently, quite simply, I will bid her good-night . . . Exactly! And she will think I am a ninny, a perfect ass, or else that I'm suffering from a pox picked up in the course of my Platonic adventures. She's taking the devil's own time over her toilette. What time is it? Ten to. Seems an endless business tonight. She has kept me waiting here several times and then packed me off after a quarter of an hour's sweet nothings; it's maddening this suspense, not knowing where one is. Leah's making a fool of me, and that's the truth of it; does she imagine I enjoy hanging about like this till her highness deigns to open the door? And I'm to play the magnanimous hero, that Galahad touch, instead of simply having a good night's love-making when I get the chance!

Damned monkey-tricks all that! Leah sends me
away because I haven't the pluck to make her keep
me; I let her play with me and then I go and invent this precious excuse that I want to win her
by forcing her admiration; why, I haven't the
guts of a schoolboy! That's enough of it; this
evening, damn it, we sleep together; it would be
too silly for words, a love affair that's been going
on so long and cost so much, to lead to nothing;
all that time and money wasted just for the pleasure of gazing at the charms of a young woman
who is playing a small part at the Nouveautés;
it's pure folly; it's worth a couple of hundred
francs and that's all; this high-falutin' business
is out of place; I know that sort of girl, exhibits
herself on the boards every night and when she's
hard up goes on duty at some establishment in
nighttown; yes, I shouldn't be a bit surprised if
she did that; with the chamber-maid on tap to
console gentlemen who have missed their turn;
the deuce take it, I've better to do with my cash
than to go buying her yards of lace for that famous
Saturday bazaar at the Continental; a fine figure
I shall cut amongst all those fellows at whom
she'll be making eyes, who'll come and drop their

cards on her next day; beastly heat and a crush of
people like that Artists' Ball where I got my hat
dinged in; and those bazaar-stalls where one is
skinned of even a cab-fare home! Confound it,
she is taking a time to-night, it's getting on my
nerves. Better knock at the door. No, can't be
done. She would try the patience of a saint. Do I
hear her moving? No, here one can't catch a sound
from the bedroom. Yes; she is opening the door.
At last!

— Well, what have you been up to, my dear?
Hope you didn't find the time too long.

Cream-white the long peignoir flows about
her, drawn in a little at the waist; but my girl is
whiter, in that creamy flowing white enfolded.

— May I come in?

— Come.

Now she is reclining in the low chair by the
fireside; white petticoats on a chair, the black
dress hanging beside them; fire nearly out; comfortable, equal warmth in the room; my hat and
coat are over there by the window; taking a low
chair, I seat myself at Leah's side; she leans back,
hands outstretched, in the blue chair with the
wide embroidered band, but for her pink cheeks

all whiteness. Against the wardrobe mirror is
set a little plush table, and on it a vague profusion
of tiny objects, boxes, scissors, ivory work,
glimmers in the clear white radiance of the room.
In warm repose, in a hush of silence, we are seated
side by side.

— You haven't told me what you did after
you left me this afternoon.

She is speaking; I answer.

— Absolutely nothing.

Stunning she looks to-night!

— Surely you dined somewhere before going
home.

— Do you want to know exactly what I did?

— Yes, do tell.

— Well, when I left you I went to see a young
gentleman, friend of mine, and strolled with him
for no less than a quarter of an hour.

She smiles.

— Did you talk to your friend about me?

— Of course.

— And your friend was very jealous, no
doubt. After that, where did you go?

Where?

— Where did I go?

Remember . . . the busy, hurrying crowd, Paris at six in the evening, streets teeming full; carriages pressing forward, held back; the Palais-Royal . . .

— I went to the Palais-Royal.

That fair woman I noticed by the Louvre shop-windows; tall, slim, alluring, haughty; lost, worse luck, for ever in the crowd.

— My friend was going to see *Ruy Blas* at the Théâtre-Français. I declined to go with him.

— All for my sake. That was heroic.

Might have been interesting to see *Ruy Blas* again; anyhow I refused; then I dined.

— I had dinner then, where was it? In one of the cafés on the Avenue de l'Opéra; you won't know it, not smart enough. Would you like to hear the menu?

— You shall tell me next time we dine together. Did you see anyone you know there?

— No one.

But there was that very pretty woman opposite, with the bald man, a lawyer or a consul, was it? That pretty, laughing woman; I wanted to see her again.

— The only people near me were a handsome

woman with an elderly gentleman who looked
like a solicitor, or a consul, perhaps.

— Congratulations.

Restful it was, my leisurely dinner in that café
gay with lights and splashes of colour, all those
strangers to watch . . . Wine, cards and women
. . . And, suddenly, a blaze of light in the nocturnal street, clear against shadows the façade of
the Eden Theatre, there I saw *Excelsior* once
with its bevy of ballet-girls; and then that good
fellow, my friend, who is going to get married;
that lucky fellow who loves and is loved.

— Nothing to relate on my way home, except
that I met a man who is loved by the girl
he loves — an event rare enough to be worth
mentioning.

— You're right; it's rare to meet a man who is
really in love.

— Do you think so?

— There are so few women a man can really
love; a woman whom many men say they love is
not loved by any of them.

Leah had no right to speak like that; but what
can I reply without offending her? Surely all,
yes all those women who have no man to love

them are unloved simply because they do not choose to be loved.

— If a woman isn't loved, I reply, it is often because she doesn't want to be.

In fact, whether it's to her credit or otherwise, a woman is always responsible for the unlove of any and every man who has seen her. There is a hint of mockery in Leah's smile; she is gazing at the dying fire; and now she looks almost exactly like her photograph.

— Did you get my note all right?

— Yes. But supposing I hadn't gone back to my place . . .

— I knew you'd go back.

— I had an hour to spare before coming to you. I spent it at home.

— What did you do?

— Nothing much; a bit of writing.

And, at my window, all that beauty of the night, the garden and the trees, those huge trees before my window, the empty, flowerless garden, vast in darkness, a fragrance of night drifting in through the open window; and, later, as I walked those empty streets and noisy boulevards, the sound of a street-organ, familiar melodies, so languorous in the darkness . . . shall I tell Leah about that?

— As I was coming here this evening, I was haunted all the way by a street-organ wailing in my ears.

— Still I know you love music.

— More than ever, less than you . . .

And her letters. *Leah d'Arsay requests Monsieur Daniel Prince* . . . Why tell Leah that I re-read her letters? She'd simply treat it as a joke; and what could I say to her about those wretched letters of hers? Or about my plan, that old idea revived, of renouncing passion for her sake? Perhaps she was right; the man who really loves is a rarity, and she has never been loved. Then . . . can it be that I, too, do not truly love her? Alas, yes, how little I love her, little indeed, for all my ideal of a perfect love!

— In fact, she says, you spent quite an enjoy-able evening.

— Quite enjoyable, in spite of a shocking lapse into unconsciousness.

She is laughing.

— And to crown it all, a delightful drive with a young lady as charming as she is unkind.

141

Unkind, that she was. And that fellow who followed us along the boulevard; the Montmartre hill outlined in mist; the row of houses with their bright windows, and trees mantled in darkness; yes, but how enchanting too she was with her assumed air of dignity, so quaintly staid! Now, too, posing no longer, she enchants me; above the pale, fluent brightness of the peignoir I am watching her head, uplifted now, palely bright; I see all the frail grace, the sinuous softness of her young body; her lips smiling appeal, a welcome to the caresses of her lover, in her soft, yielding poise a promise of surrender; for in this hour when day is spent and ended, after the passing of the futile day, night is come at last; love's own hour. . . . Oh love, my love, your lips are gossamer . . . lightly wafted afar . . . on the winds of night . . .

And her hands; from her hands, through mine, my arms, my breast, is borne a thrill, a warmth, an immanence of desire that rises vibrant to my swooning eyes. Good-bye to all delays of deference and humble passion, to those fine projects for a slowly perfected love, evasions and renouncement. I'm done with renunciation; I will

have her to-night! My eyes are held by that
sensual pallor of her, promising delight; no
longer will I renounce her for a dream's sake. But
now she withdraws her hands from mine and I
move back, two paces back; she comes to me,
places her hands upon my shoulders and, as I
grow intoxicated, maddened by their contact,
she speaks:
— You'll come next Saturday to the bazaar
at the Continental, won't you? You'll see me at
my best.
No doubt.
— I shall be awfully upset if you don't put in
an appearance; I shall make a great fuss of you,
you'll see.
Really!
— Now mind you bring me that apron for my
dress.
Her dress? Yes, that apron . . . and the money
I promised, why, I'd forgotten all about it, she
wants it now; I promised; anyhow, it's the least
I can do. Here goes, let's get it over!
— If you will tell me, Leah, about how much
it will come to, and excuse me for asking you to
see about it yourself . . .

— I can't say exactly. It would be. Well, not more than a hundred francs.

— Here it is.

I have a fifty-franc note in my card-case, and some louis in my purse, only twenty-franc pieces; that'll make a hundred and ten francs; oh, all right; three louis and fifty francs, there, on the mantelpiece.

— It's very nice of you, Leah says.

She comes back; I have pleased her; a bit expensive it was; still she will be kind now, show her appreciation; this way, too, I feel less compunction about staying the night, in fact she owes it to me; anyhow, surely I can prove my love to her without declining the gift of herself; for tonight I will love her so gently, so tenderly and so fondly, that it will be better than all the set speeches and renunciations in the world; in fact, if I go the right way about it, by spending the night with her I shall be able far better to prove to her the sincerity of my love; yes, that's what I must do; and I whisper into her hair.

— Then . . . I stay to-night?

Her big eyes, her eyes amazed, pitying almost they seem . . . ah, what am I to read in them?

— No, not to-night, really not to-night. I
can't . . .

Why? Not to-night? She refuses?

— Next time, I promise you . . . I can't, oh,
I can't . . .

Again, she refuses again? I can't compel her.
No, she means No.

— Oh Leah, won't you let me . . . ?

— I swear that . . .

What use insisting?

— Then . . . good-night.

Oh why did I ask her? Why didn't I hold to
my resolve and leave her, as I should have done,
with flags flying?

— Good-night, dear.

I kiss her forehead; ah that delight impossible,
elusive; fatal, desperate delight!

— Come Wednesday at three, she says.

— Delighted.

Why, oh why did I again try to possess her?
Once more she has eluded me. Must go; my
coat, hat.

— Au revoir, she says. Wednesday at three.

Holding the candlestick, she opens the drawing-room door; Marie appears; we cross the hall.

— Wednesday then, at three, I say.

No, I will never see her again; never again must I see her; what use would it be? All is over now and done with, all possibility of love between us, and I look on her beauty, her white unforgettable beauty, as now she holds out her hand.

— *Au revoir.*

— *Au revoir.*

Friendly she smiles *au revoir*, while lambent on her bosom flickers the pale nocturnal light.

New Directions Paperbooks – A Partial Listing

For complete listing request free catalog from
New Directions, 80 Eighth Avenue, New York 10011

† Bilingual

For complete listing request free catalog from
New Directions, 80 Eighth Avenue, New York 10011   † Bilingual